MORE THAN FOUR

Maggie Skull

contents

Four and no more

***"Ugh my head. What the hell happened?"Forcing my eyes opened and taking in my surroundings, I'm lost. This is not my bed. Not my room. The rooms old and dusty. There's a small window with the moonlight casting a glow in the room. It smells of old books and vanilla? That can't be right?

Getting out of bed. The floor is hardwood and cold. I can't wrap my head around what's going on. How did I get here? Where is here anyway?

A small light is casting under a door with dust bunnies floating in the air. I stumble to door and thank everything that's holy, it's unlocked. The door creaks and cobwebs fall off from the opening.

I enter a hallway. It's cold and drafty. There's a light ahead. Might as well go there. I think. I enter an open space with a living room and kitchen combined. It's clean and smells of vanilla.

"Someone must be cooking?"

But there's no one in here. I creep to the center of room. Trying to be quiet thinking if I was kidnapped no sense in letting them know I'm here and out of my drafty room.

Suddenly a guy. A well built guy at that, comes stumbling in the room. He looks at me stunned. Guess I'm looking the same way. Stunned and very confused.

"Who the hell are you?" He said. "Me? Who the hell are you?" I mean, come on. I'm the one standing here in my pajamas and cold as fuck! Why is he being rude?

"Where am I?" He said. Then I get a good look at him. He's very handsome. Beautiful brown eyes. Great body. Standing there in just his boxers and looking good enough to lick.

Stop it Kyra! He could be your kidnapper and your drooling over the over the guy. What the hell am I thinking?

"I'm Kyra, and you are?" Though if he is my kidnapper he should know that already, right? I'm clueless and really freaking cold.

"Uhm I'm Julian. Julian Black.""Where am I?" "How did I get here?"

A door slams behind us and another guy comes stumbling in with his hair a mess and grumbling foul words. There's blood on the side of his head, running down his face. He's big and obviously pissed.

"What the fuck is going on?" He whimpers. It's barely above a whisper but I heard him. He looks up, clearly shocked and disoriented. Seeing us in the room he walks over to Julian, grabbing him by his neck and lifting him off the floor with little ease.

"WHY AM I HERE?, WHO THE FUCK ARE YOU!" Boy is he pissed. Julian's grasping and turning red, not able to talk.

"Stop! You big beast! Let him go!" Running over to help Julian, though I don't know why, I don't even know the guy. But he didn't seem like he deserved to be choked out by the big burly beast.

I get knocked on my ass for the effort though. These guys are huge. Then two men come running seemingly out of nowhere and knock the beast to floor. Making a Julian fall to the floor in a very ungracious way. It would be comical if it wasn't so scary. The big three land in a human pile beside me and my very bruised ego and butt.

The beast is calming down but still agitated and confused, like all of us here no doubt. I need answers and I'm fed the fuck up!!

"Look, I know we're all confused and tired. But in no way is choking out Julian over here gonna get us any answers.""So can we please all calm the fuck down and talk!"

They all look at me like I'm the one who's insane. Well maybe I am. Waking up in a strange bed and in strange place after an earthquake, does seem insane. But then we're all here so can we all be insane at once? Who knows? Maybe? I have no clue and I'm done being nice.

"Ok look, why don't we just sit down and talk. Find out how and why were here. You know? Act like adults and not moronic beast!"

The two guys who stormed beast look at me and smile. Devilishly I might add. Ones tattooed from neck to chest. Good looking and sexy. The other is just as sexy but with a boyish charm. Get your damn head out of the gutter Krya! They could be killers. Your killers! Ugh!

"Ok temptress, let's talk." Said tattoo guy, with a sly smirk. What the..? He's a playboy also and damn if it isn't hot.

"Ok, let's set at the island in the kitchen and calmly talk about this.. well situation we're in, shall we?" Getting off the floor with a grimace. Damn my butt hurts.

We all pile around the island. It's cracked but clean. White and big. Enough to for all five of us to sit around comfortably. I sit and Mr. Tattoo crashes beside me. The other side sets beast and the rest get settled all around.

"Ok let's start at the beginning and please inside voices." I laugh what the hell am I doing? And what have I gotten myself into?

Jaxson

Damn my head! Where the hell am I? Waking up in a bed that's not my own isn't uncommon but usually there's a chick beside me and I'm usually hungover. But this isn't a hangover. The last thing I remember was being at the club getting shit faced with my buddies. The entire bar starting shaking and now here I am. Not drunk or happily laid. Waking up with a pounding headache and in a strange place.

I hear a scream. Scaring the shit out of me. I jump out of bed and run in the direction of the scream. Bumping into another guy headed in the same direction. Stopping in our tracks we see a beast of a man strangling a guy from his neck, helplessly dangling off of the floor. There's a babe trying to get him off of him but not succeeding. She's a tiny thing and beautiful. Long brown hair and a sexy as hell body.

I hear a grunt from the dangling guy and jump into action.

We jump into gear and tackle the beast to the ground. Damn took two of us. This guy is huge. Banged my knee on the way down. I look up over the pile of bodies I'm on top of and see the most sexy woman sitting beside us. She has beautiful honey brown eyes with the cutest little nose and pink puffed out lips that's very sexy and drool worthy. Her body is rocking and to die for and I think I'm half in love already. I scramble up off of the pile quickly.

She gets us to sit at the island and talk our situation out. I'm half listening. I can't keep my eyes off her. Her lips are moving and I'm transfixed on how plump and fuckable they are and not the conversation. Shit! I need to pay attention.

"My names Kyra Grace. I don't know how I got here. I was asleep coming off a twelve hour shift. The bed starting shaking. Then I blacked out and woke up here. Wherever here is? What about y'all?" She has a little country twang which makes her even more adorable.

" I'm Jaxson, just call me Jax. I was at a club with my buddies getting drunk. The bar started shaking and I woke up here. I have no idea how I got here or how." I said looking at all the guys and lastly her. Kyra, what a pretty name for a such a sexy chic. She's like my dream girl all wrapped up in a steamy hot package.

"I'm Julian Black, I just got off work. I was in bed also the bed starting shaking then I ended up here. At first I thought I was dreaming. Now

I know it's just a damn nightmare!" He said with a grimace. Can't blame him. If it wasn't for the temptress setting next to me I think it was a nightmare too.

"I'm Tuck, I was just getting out of the shower with my girlfriend and the room starting shaking. I got hit in on the head by falling debris and ending up here. Maybe I got a concussion or something I don't know. This doesn't make any damn sense." The beast says though I understand where he's coming from. None of this makes fucking sense.

"I'm Damon Knight I was at a gas station. Same as all of you the ground starts shaking and I wake up here. Confused and cold. Has anyone checked if there's more people here? Are we the only ones?"

Damn didn't think of that. "Well we can split up and check all the rooms. Check the surrounding area outside. Try to get a feel of where we are." My little temptress says damn she's cute.

"Good idea! Let's go in teams instead. Don't know where we are or what we may come across." Says the beast or Tuck. What kind of name is Tuck anyway?

"I'll go with temptress here. We can check all the rooms on this floor." I don't want her out of my sight. She's to tiny to go anywhere alone. I'm in protective mode and she's a damsel in distress. I need to get a hold of my self and start thinking rationally.

"Ok let's go. The sooner the better. My damn head hurts." Said beast no Tuck damn. Then we head off in search of others or to get some idea as to what the hell is going on. Letting the little temptress walk in front of me. Damn she has a fine ass. I think I'm in trouble here.

Kyra

Temptress really? Well could be worse. He's not bad on the eyes either. We go to each room. Some are dusty and smelly and some are very clean a completely different contrast. There's about five bedrooms. A kitchen and living room open space. Utility room and two bathrooms just on this floor alone. This place is huge. There's a sliding glass door that opens to a very big and surprisingly clean pool.

"Nice strange how some parts of this house looks new and some old right? But the pool is nice at least there's that." Said Jax with another sexy smirk. Get your head in the game Kyra can't go all horny teenager on these guys. Damn but oh if only.

"There's a shed over here, let's check it out." He said

"Uhm you go ahead. I'm not a big fan of snakes or spiders or serial killers for that matter. Looking in a lonely shed only invites trouble." I mean really I may be clueless but not that damn clueless. I half laugh.

"Oh come on temptress I'll protect you." There he goes again with the temptress, wtf?"Why do you call me that? Temptress I mean?" He smiles that sexy smile that has me drooling.

"Because your are a very tempting and sexy woman. Why else?" Yea right. Me? You got to be kidding. I'm not tempting and nowhere near sexy. I'm just a a twenty one year old cashier and part time student. All alone and fighting tooth and nail for scraps and bill money. I'm not a temptress. I'm nobody.

"Well stop it! I'm not a temptress, I'm nobody. Just lost and very confused at the moment." And apparently very horny. Get a grip Kyra!

"Ah no temptress you're not a nobody and we're all confused at the moment. Doesn't look like anyone else is here. At least on this floor. Let's go back the kitchen and see if the others found anything." Sure why not at least being around the others will get my mind off the handsome tattoo man who is making my hot pocket go wild. Headed to the kitchen/living room he place his hand on my back sending little tingles all over me. I can not be attracted to this guy. Get your head in the game. Damn!Going into the kitchen no one but us here. So I decide to keep busy and check the fridge and cabinets. Fully stocked to the rim. Uh? It's like someone knew we were gonna be here. Very confusing and has me wondering if this is sort of a kidnapping situation. I'm checking my room or at least the room

I woke up in. As I head to the room Jax is on my heels. I light up the room running over to the closet and I'm shook. There's clothes tons of clothes and all in my size. Plus shoes of all kinds. I run over to the dresser and yes tons of underwear and even negligees. Socks, pantyhose, and a damn vibrator! I mean really. I run the the adjacent bathroom and yes yet again fully stocked even has tampons and condemns. Wtf!!

"What's going on? We're fully stocked. To the hilt. I have clothes and shoes my size. Even damn tampons! We're fully stocked on food and drinks! It's like this was planned!" This shit is really getting on my nerves.

"Calm down Kyra I'm sure there's a reasonable explanation. Right?"Yea right. We go into the kitchen where the others are finally back. Looking displeased and as confused as I am.

"Well did you find anyone or anything?" I mean I'm at my breaking point. No need to be nice. "No we didn't find a damn thing. But we all have clothes and all the necessities they we need. Some rooms are empty though. Seems like someone planned for us to be here. Why I don't know?" Said Julian running his hand through his hair and grunting out his displeasure.

"Well I guess we're totally fucked then." And boy are we.

TUCK

Why me? I never asked for this shit. I just need to get back home. Back to Candance. My beautiful and shy little princess. Making love in the shower one minute and the next it all turns to shit. If I don't get back soon my damn brother is gonna move in on Candance. He's always wanted her and be damn if I'm giving him the opportunity to stake his claim. Though Candance has always had a soft spot for Chuck my twin. I don't think she would ever act on those feelings. Right? Crap! I so need need to get back. This couldn't happen at worse time either. I just got the job at the Shady Lounge as a bouncer and after the fiasco of my last job. I so need to get back. There's no doubt in that. I've been trying to change for her. Only her. She wanted me to be more. So I'm trying. Dammit I'm trying! But the longer I'm here the more scared I am the she will leave me for him. My damn brother!

"We need to come up with a plan to get the hell out of here. Has anyone checked their cellphones? Is there any service? Any connection with anybody?" I can't believe this.

"I don't have mine. I was in bed. It's still on its charger, I think." Said Kyra. Her voice is so soft you could barely hear her. Worry all over her beautiful face. I feel her pain I don't have my phone either. I was in the shower for fuck sakes.

"I left mine in the car while I was in the station. What about you?" Damon I think his name is ask Jax. Dudes got a lot of damn tattoos all over him. That must of hurt. I have one but nothing compared to him.

"Nope sorry didn't carry it to the club always too noisy and I'm presuming you don't have yours either. Huh Julian? Since you were in bed also."

"Nope sure don't. What are we gonna do now?" Julian ask and sure don't have any answers. Wish I did though. This is a headache. I swipe the dried blood off my face.

"Well is there a television? Maybe we can check to see some news broadcast or something than tell us what is going on? I hope anyway. The sooner the better we can get the hell out of here. Kyra goes to turn turn tv on. Hell I didn't even notice it. She bends over looking for the buttons and damn if my dick didn't just get hard. She's got a nice ass I can say that about her. The tv comes on and all we see snow. Shit! She clicks more buttons but still nothing. Well there goes that.

"Sorry guys. Nothing. How about a radio? Anybody see one of those while we were looking around?" Great idea I think I did somewhere in one the musty rooms upstairs.

"Hold on I'll go check." As I run up the stairs to find the dang radio. Now which room was it? Oh yea third door down. Damn why does this place smell like vanilla? I found it on the side table. Dusting of the dirt as I go back I see it has a plug at least. That's good. In the living room looking for a plug I find behind the table. Turning it on and yep all static. Fuck! Now what? The gloom in everyone's faces tells me they feel the same way I do. Lost.

" I guess will have to wait till morning to look around. See if there's anyone around. Look for a car or something. Till then we should get some sleep." She's right I guess but I so wanted to get out of her now not later.

"Yeah sounds like I plan I'm tired and so need to sleep this nightmare off." Says Julian though I agree on the nightmare part. I don't think sleep will be coming tonight. I look at the big clock above the tv and groan. Man it's three in the morning. Guess I do need sleep.

"Hey temptress wanna share a bed with me? I'll play nice. Just wanna cuddle." Pfft I doubt she's up for that.

"No thanks big guy think I can handle a room and bed all on my own." She half laughs. I wouldn't mind a cuddle buddy myself but I'm not stepping in that puddle. I have to think about Candance and getting back home to her.

"Well I'm off. If this is a nightmare it was nice meeting you all and have a good life." Said Damon. Cheeky bastard. Winking at Kyra as he walks by. No doubt wishing she was in his bed as well.

"Night folks and please don't wake me. I'm not early bird." Julian said as he walks off claiming a room.

"Night guys. If we're all still here in the morning I'll cook breakfast. Then we can get to work figuring out how to get y'all home." Notice she didn't say get her home. Interesting.

"Ok but the offer still stands temptress. You know if you get lonely." He smiles and scoffs as she walks off headed to the room she woke up in I guess. Nice to watch her walk away though. Jax takes off claiming his room as well and I'm stuck here by myself praying I can find a way to get the hell out here before morning. No way I wanna stay and end up being tempted by Jax's so called temptress. Guess I'll find a flashlight and head outside to look around. Nowhere near tired and really to anxious to sleep. Just hoping against hope that I can find a way out of here.

Fuck! Hold on Candance baby I will find a way home. I hope.

Julian

Trying to sleep in a bed other than my own is useless. Tossing and turning and feeling anxious I decide to give it up and snoop. I take off back through the kitchen and grab me a water from the fridge. I'm so damn bored and since I'm usually a night owl being up this late isn't unusual. The house is eerily quiet and for some reason I find it comforting. Going to the couch I slam down on it and try to get comfortable. Noticing some dvds beside the tv I decided to watch one. Not a big selection but at least it's something. I see Magic Mike in the slim collection and pop it in. Since I'm a stripper I can learn from some of the techniques not watching it because of the guys just a learning video for me.

I hear someone come up behind me and turn and notice it's Tuck looking worn out and frustrated. The guy is unique to say the least. He's huge for all accounts. I'm a big guy at 6'2 but he seems to be a mountain compared to me.

"Magic Mike really? Something you wanna tell me Julian?" I laugh no doubt he's thinking I'm gay. Far from it but I'll enlighten him.

"Yea just learning some new moves. I'm a stripper heard the techniques were good." Laughing he sits besides me. "Maybe you can get me a job, pretty sure mine is no longer available." Probably not but I may not have mine as well. This shit show is a major fuck up. Grunting I just go back to watching the movie.

We hear a door creak open looking over we see Kyra entering the kitchen in a daze. She looks like she just woke up with a hair in a mess and cute little pajama short and tops that's quite close to being see through. Not that I'm complaining she looks really desirable.

"Morning guys." She said as she yawns and stretches showing off her midriff and cute little belly button piercing. Man she's hot. Being here with just her and three guys is going to be tempting and hard as fuck. No wonder Jax calls her temptress. She seems innocent too. Can't understand how a woman these days could be that sexy and never been touched. But to each his own I guess.

"Good morning Kyra." Tuck states with a gruff. What's wrong this guy? I know it's a crappy situation but theres no need to be rude.

"How about some breakfast?" "You guys hungry?" Yea I am but not for what she has in mind. I clear my throat trying to escape from my sinful thoughts about her. Man it's to soon to be thinking this shit.

"Yea cookie breakfast sounds good." She looks at me a bit put off but turns and starts cooking. I walk over to the island and offer her help but she declines. So I set and watch her cook and trying to refrain myself from looking at her sweet ass. I'm sexually frustrated and just need to release the tension from aching cock. That's all this is. I'm use to having sex often. A stripper usually gets a lot of opportunities and I usually take every advantage thrown my way but lately I haven't been doing it. It's just grown to seem meaningless and devoid of any feelings. I mean I'm still young I'm only 32 but casual sex just isn't doing it for me anymore. Well I say casual but I've done a lot in the sexual department. Threesomes, foursomes, hell I even done Bdsm. But none that is doing it for me anymore. I just feel lost lately. Now I'm really lost. Don't know where I am. Hell don't even know when I am. But at least I got a good view.

"Something smells good. Ahh my little temptress cooking for her men. Why thank you darling." Jax laughs as he grabs the bacon off the plate. Dressed in towel but nothing else.

"Put some damn clothes on dude. Not everybody wants to see that!" Tuck complains from the couch still watching the movie. Ha now who looks gay. Nothing against the lifestyle it's just not for me.

"Considering what your watching I beg to disagree. You know you like looking at my sexy body baby!" Hollers Jax with a loud laugh.

"I wasn't watching it dear Julian over there put it on. Not me!" "Hey was watching to learn Tuck not admiring their contributes." I laugh Tuck clearly flustered at being caught.

"You're a stripper?" A soft voice whispers at my ear. I turn and smile at Kyra raising my eyebrows up and down. "Yes honey wanna show?" She looks surprised at my question and quickly recovers leaning closer she said "Anytime" which shocks the shit out of me. Here I was thinking she was totally innocent. "Sweetheart I'll give you the best performance of your lifetime."

She walks away laughing. Now I'm really confused is she innocent or not? Either way I'm intrigued. I look at her laughing and notice she has dimples. Deep beautiful dimples when she smiles. Cutest thing I've ever seen. Yea I need to go relieve some tension and soon.

"Breakfast is done. Better get it before Jax eats it all." Looking at Jax scarfing down his food like he's never ate a day in his life. We all get to situated and start eating. Damn the best breakfast I ever tasted. "This is really good Krya, thank you."There goes those dimples again and wham I'm instantly hard. She's driving me nuts.

"Ok so why don't we get to know each other since you know we're stuck together. For a while at least." Kyra ask oh ok sounds good why not?

"I'll start. I'm Julian as you know. I'm 32 a stripper. I love movies, reading, and uhm women." Laughing at myself.

"Tuck, girlfriend Candance, brother Chuck. I'm 30. I love working out at the gym, fishing, and guns." No surprise there.

"I'm Damon I own a few businesses. I'm 31. I love clubs, money, and of course women." Hell I didn't even notice him come in. Sneaky bastard. He's quite and a bit overwhelming. I've seen him somewhere before just can't place him. He has that gangster vibe going on. Never says much always listening though.

"Jax I'm the prez of the local MC the Devils Demons. Im 28 love motorcycles, working on cars, and sex!!" No surprise there either.

"Ok well I'm Kyra. Im 21. Im a cashier and part time student. Im into art, theater, and music. Im studying art at Granville East Art school." Wow yea color me surprised there. Very artistic wonder what she intends to do with the art degree? Not many jobs in the field. But hey I'm a stripper so who am I to question it.

"What are you gonna do with an art degree? I don't see many opportunities in that these days?" Tuck ask. My thoughts exactly.

"Well I'm going to open a tattoo shop or plan to anyway. I've always loved drawing. Im pretty good at it and it's always been my dream.

There may not be too many opportunities for an art student but I intend to make a go at it." Good for her. I'd love to see her drawings.

"Got any tats on you temptress?" "I would love to see them. You know to give you my honest opinion. Then maybe you can do one for me." Jax as usual trying to charm her. "Yes I have one that I did on myself but it's not in an appropriate place to show you. Yet." She laughs hmmm sounds interesting. Wouldn't mind seeing for myself. Geez enough man I so need a shower.

"Im off to take a shower then. Thank you for breakfast cookie it was delicious." Headed to the shower and a release but I could've sworn on my way there I heard Jax laughing his creepy laugh. Bastard.

Damon

I'm sitting in the living room getting impatient wanting out of this hell hole we're in. I really don't like these mother fuckers much. These people aren't my type that I associate with. I feel like killing them all and being done with it. I'm not a nice guy and never had been. I have deep dark secret and I'm a damn monster. I don't need this shit. The only bright spot in this dim place is her. But she's not enough to keep my thoughts occupied and my demons at bay.

I have to get back to reality before I lose my mind. I have a businesses to run. Responsibilities and a gang to get back to and quick. Before Marco gets it in his head to try and take over my shit. The bastard has been a bane In my side for years. Always trying to take over my territory and turn others against me. It's time to get out of here.

"I'm tired of this shit, I'm going to look around the town and see if I find anything or anyone. Someone wanna come with?" The sooner the better.

"Sure I'll go with you I want out of this place like now." Tuck said after grabbing a water and headed for the door.

"I'll hang back with temptress, don't want to leave her alone." Of course not. "Hell no! I'm going to just hang on." As she grabs a pair of sunglasses and bolts off around Jax. "Guess we're all going." Said Julian with a huff.

Leaving are so called homestead we head out. Two hours later we come trudging back in. All we seen is empty abandon buildings and not a damn soul in sight. It's like it's a damn ghost town. The buildings looked old and it's all dusty like we're in an old western movie. My temper is on high. Im tired, dirty, and fed up! We all are and looks like there's no way back home. I grab my switchblade out and start playing with it trying to ease my anger but it's not helping. I want to hit something or someone. We're all on edge and this shit isn't funny anymore.

"What now? This is a nightmare come true. It's outrageous and I'm at a complete loss. I don't know what do? Im gonna lose my job. My house. My school placement. Everything. This can not be happening. Someone please wake me up!" We all feel the same. Wish I could get her back. She looks so sad and lost. We all do. But these people aren't my problem.

"Look at this way cookie you have us and we all feel the same way but at least we're not alone." Julian always the peace maker. How is this guy a stripper? Such a damn softie.

"Well I for one am not giving up! I will find a way out of this place. Even it kills me! This is complete and utter bullshit! I feel like I'm in the damn Twilight Zone!" Of course Tuck is showing his aggravation he always does. Guys got a temper. He's getting on my damn nerves. Maybe I should kill his ass first. I hate the way my mind goes down these roads all the time. Damn I need beer.

"Got any beer in this place I need to get completely drunk to deal with you fuckers!"

I make my way to the kitchen. Slamming the fridge open. Yes! There on the bottom shelf is a six pack of cold beer now all I need is a blunt and some good pussy. I look over to Kyra. Wonder what she's in to? Nah to innocent I don't do virgins. Too messy. But damn she looks good. Yea I really need to get high.

"Hand me one of those will ya?" Jax of course. Guys way too happy to be here. Makes me nervous. I hand him a beer and go back to the couch. This is useless. We need to get a grip and try to come to terms with what's going on and figure this shit out. We're getting nowhere this way.

"Guys we need to calm our heads and think clearly and work this out. Yelling is not getting us anywhere. Arguing is not getting us anywhere. Somehow, some way, we need to regroup and think rationally. There has to be a reason and a way." I try to relax and think logically. It happened with the quake. That much we know. It happened at night and it seems it only happened to us, but why? That's the question. Why just us? Four men and one girl who basically don't even know each other and have absolutely nothing in common I don't think any of us truly want to be here. Maybe it's the Gods playing tricks on us. Maybe it's purgatory. Maybe we're all crazy? Who the hell knows?

Kyra sits besides me and grabs my hand. Wtf? She looks at me and sighs and then grants me one of her beautiful smiles.

"It's going to be ok. We will get through this. We will find a way home. I have absolute faith in that."Is she crazy? Beautiful but crazy. I pull my hand back.

"I don't like to be touched!" I quip.

"Oh sorry" she gives me sad look and walks off. Damn why did I say that? Wasn't trying to be rude but I really don't like someone's hands on me. Unless I give them permission of course. I'm fucked up that way.

"I'm sorry Kyra. I didn't mean to upset you. I just have..well I have.
.this condition that is.." fuck I can't even talk.

"It's ok I understand." She smiles and walks off. Damn I'm an idiot.
It's my demons I just can't get close to anybody. I've tried. I truly have.
I can't even let someone touch me during sex. I have to have control.
But she didn't know that. I'm an ass. I get up and walk over to her at
the island and sit down. I hate that I upset her. It bothers me. I hate
when women cry or suffer even if it's my doing. I sigh.

"Look Krya it's not you, it's me. I'm messed up. I've well, I've been
through a lot and have issues. Please forgive me. I didn't mean to
sound rude." Luckily she smiles at me and tells me it's fine and doesn't
Try to touch me again. But I feel bad. I get up and head to my room. I
need to get away. I don't why but when I'm around her I find it hard
to breathe. Me and my fucked up past. Can't even be touched by a
woman. How messed up is that? I crash down on my bed throwing
my empty beer bottle across the room, I close my eyes and drift off
into a restless sleep.

Kyra

S ix weeks! Six long exasperated weeks! We've been stuck here and still no progress. No one's getting along. We fight. We yell. We're exhausted and the pressure isn't easing up. Everyday it's the same routine. We get up, we eat, we scavenger the streets and the buildings. Getting further and further away with each day and still nothing. We come back, we mope, we complain, we get on each other's nerves. We eat then bed. All to do it over again and again. I'm done. I can't take anymore. The guys can't seem to relax. It's putting me on edge and sexual tension does not help. Jax is the worst. Constantly teasing and flirting. It's driving me mad! I need an escape. I need a break. I need out of here! Ugh!

Suddenly arms wrap around my waist and kisses are making its way down my neck.

"Come on cookie it could be worse." Oh yes Julian he's always rubbing me and touching me whenever he can. Not that I don't enjoy the attention, who wouldn't? They're all sexy and good looking men. But I know it's because I'm the only girl here. If we're back home these men would not give me a second look. I'm not the kind that attracts guys like these. My confidence level is not up to theirs. I'm just me. Nothing special. So their attention is misplaced. I'm just not their type of girl. I accept that. Why can't they? I remove myself from his grasp and step away.

"Stop doing that! You're always touching me. It confuses me. God I wish I wasn't the only girl here. You guys would never give me single glance if you met me in the streets! You only do it because I'm the only female here! It's not fair!" I'm emotional I know but they can't keep torturing me like this.

"What are you talking about cookie? Of course I would notice you. Just look at you. You're beyond beautiful. Just not on the outside but on the inside too!" I look down at myself. Ripped crop jeans and a cut off shirt. Belly piercing and a bit of tan. My stomach is flat but I worked damn hard for that. In school I was the pudgy kid with braces. I grew into my height which is not saying much cause I stand at 5'3. But it's still far from from beautiful. I wish I could see what they do.

"Just leave me alone. I need fresh air!" I go to leave and run smack into the beast. Nearly falling over.

"Woah sorry there sugar didn't see you." What the...the beast is being nice. He even apologized. I stand on my tiptoes and place my hand on his forehead. "What are you doing?" He ask. "Seeing if you have fever. You're being nice. What's wrong?" He laughs then smiles. The beast actually smiled. I'm in shock. Miracles do happen it seems.

"I can be nice sugar, when I want to be. Why are you in such rush?" Ugh men they're so confusing. "I need some air. I'm going for a walk. I'll be back soon." I head for the sliding door to get away from all these emotions that keep tormenting me.

"Not alone your not. There's no telling what's out there and you shouldn't be by yourself just in case." I look at him like he lost his damn mind. I'm a grown ass women. I just turn and take off. Who do they think they are? Almost to door someone grabs my arm I look to see Damon with a fierce look on his face. He's touching me. He doesn't liked to be touch but he can touch me? Oh hell no!

"You're touching me Damon. Isn't that against the rules?" He laughs. It's sexy when he laughs he rarely does it. "No spitfire I can touch but you can't." Double standard I think. I yank out of his grasp and take off running for the door. I run into the empty street and stop.

I'm looking around and it's still the same old buildings same lonely street. I take off walking and decide to try entering the buildings. I'm a snoop and bored so why not? I notice a building on my right that I haven't seen before. Strange it's like it just appeared. It looks a lot newer than the others. I go to open the door but it's stuck. I slam my body into it and it breaks open. That's gonna hurt later. I enter the building and I hear music. What? Music? The sound seems so out of place. I haven't heard music in awhile. I search for a light switch and find it on the east wall. Illuminating the room I look around in shock. It's a bar. An outdated bar but clean. There's a jukebox in the corner playing. That explains the music. I recognize the song it's Lost in your eyes I think it's by Debbie Gibson.

Looking around I see liquor bottles on shelves an old type of register on the wooden bar and soft round stools in front. Empty tables all around and the smell cigars in the air. Cigars? That can't be right. I take off running back to the house as I exit the building. I have to tell the guys. I crash in the house out of air. Trying to catch my breath and look around at the quizzical faces. "I found..a..bar.. I try to wheeze out. Jax brings me a water and tells me to calm down. Taking breathes in and out finally catching my breath I scream out"THERES A BAR!" they looked at each other surely thinking I've gone mad. It is kind of comical.

"Woah sugar just explain. Deep breathes. That's it. Now what are you talking about." It still feels strange that he's being nice. "There's a new building. It's a bar it just appeared out of nowhere. Come look!" I run out hoping they follow as I get to the spot the building is gone. It's back to the basic old crumpled building that was there before. What the?"No it was here I swear. It had a jukebox and lots of liquor and I swear it was here. It was here! I'm losing my damn mind!" I throw the water bottle at the building. Water splashes on the door and it flickers. It flickered! Then the building transforms back to the bar I saw previously. "See I told you! I'm not crazy! Go inside and look!"

We open the door and go inside the song has changed on the jukebox playing a Duran Duran song. The one about the wolves. I love eighties music. I look at the guys who are looking around in awe. I laugh I knew I wasn't crazy. "Looks like you were right spitfire a damn bar. Where did it come from?" Damon ask more to hisself than us. We're all amazed and start looking around. I go to side door and open it, it squeaks as I open it. I notice it's a full blown kitchen though outdated. I walk over to the fridge open it and yea it's fully stocked. I notice a staircase off to the side. I start to call out to one of the guys but decide against it and walk up the stairs alone. At the top of the staircase there's a red door that's cracked open. I open it and beyond the door is a fully furnished apartment with old furniture but it's clean. There's a side door I open and it leads to bedroom. Big queen size bed in center and dressers on the side. Another door I'm presuming leads to the bathroom is on the far wall. I go look through the dressers and find eighty style clothes. Fishnet stocking, faded ice jeans, and neon shirts. Under a shirt I find a bag a weed and papers. Jackpot! The guys will love this. I pocket the weed and go back to the livingroom area. Crashing yet again into Tuck. For a big guy he's quite as hell. He catches me before I stumble backwards. He's big beefy hands grabbing my hips and pulling me forwards. Crashing into his big muscled body. He groans and rubs his hands on my sides. Before I get lost in the heat of the moment I pull back and look up at him. He is handsome. His big beautiful brown eyes looks down at me and smiles. I get tingles just from his smile alone and lost in eyes. He clears his throat and let's me go stepping back a bit. "Sorry again. You seem to keep bouncing into me today. I'm not complaining though." He raises his hand and his finger traces my jawline and goes down my neck. Sending pure pleasure through me. I moan and he drops his his hand. Sad from the loss of contact I step aside and start looking around.

"I found a little surprise for later hidden in the dresser. You guys just might like it." I laugh and go back down the stairs. I find the rest sitting at the bar drinking and laughing. It's good to see them this way. I'm almost glad I found the place. I go to join them and get me a drink also. "Why don't we grab a few bottles and head back home. Have a little party and loosen up a bit? What ya think?" Hoping we can relieve some tension of the last six weeks and just relax. I so need it. I know they do too.

"Sounds like a plan cookie. Jax grab some bottles and Damon grab some glasses." As Julian grabs some whiskey and rum I think. I'm not much of a drinker. It's not gonna take much to get me drunk. But I do smoke weed and can't wait till we get this party started.

We head out back home. Home huh? I guess it has become sort of a home for us. I decide to just relax and see where the night takes me. I'm tired of being frustrated and mad. I need cut loose and just enjoy myself. As we head into our home, I can't wait to just cut loose for once in my life.

Famous last words.

Jax

Yes party time! Man I missed this. Friends, we'll sort of, good booze and the chance of being with a pretty little temptress. Life is so good. "Look what I found." Kyra places the baggie and papers on the table. Damn I'm in heaven now. "Yes my temptress, I so love you." She gives me a big smile. Damn those dimples.

"Anyone got a lighter?" I reach in my pocket and pull out the gem. Laughter goes around. Tuck sets in the chair in the corner. Damon,Krya, and Julian are the couch and I set on the chair next to them. Liquor and weed on the table. Hell if we only had music it would be perfect. Damon starts to roll a couple of joints as Julian pours out the liquor. Tuck seems to be in a better mood today. The grouch needed to lighten up. We're all tossing back drinks and puffing away. I feel my buzz kicking in, this is pure bliss.

"Let's play a game." Julian says he's high as fuck right now. "Ok what game?" As I take another drag. "How about truth or dare?" Is he kidding.

"What are we 12?" I ask laughing. "Oh come on it will be fun, I'll start." He said eyes as red as blood. I look around and everyone is loaded and feeling all kinds of happy. "Sure why not, begin oh master of games." He laughs. Takes a drink then looks at Kyra this should be good.

"Cookie truth or dare?" She thinks on it then giggles "dare" brave girl. Julian smiles "I dare you to kiss Tuck." Wtf? No way is Tuck going to go for that. Kyra looks and Tuck and smiles. He looks tense. Interesting. Will she do it? She gets up walks to him and pecks him on check. "No way, full blown kiss or you don't get to drink or smoke." Said Julian she huffs then turns and actually lays one on him and hard. Tuck grabs the back of her head and pulls her in and the kiss gets deeper. He moans and Kyra breaks the kiss fully flushed. Damn my dick is hard.

"Fuck" Damon grunts. My thoughts exactly. She turns and sits back down. "Julian truth or dare?" Kyra ask. "Dare of course, who wimps out and chooses truth?" He laughs "I dare you to strip." "Down to your boxers." She adds. Of course Julian does. Putting a little emphasis on his show for her. The dudes got balls. We all laugh. He sits back down. My turn. "Truth or dare Damon?" "Dare" he says ok what to dare? I got it. "I dare you to hotbox Kyra." Simple enough. He turns to Kyra and damn if the fucker didn't make it sensual as hell. Now my dicks even harder.

"Truth or dare Tuck?" Said Damon. "Dare" nobodies going with truth. Don't wanna spill no beans I guess. "I dare you remove Kyras shirt." He laughs. Dude is high. Tuck gnaws he jaws. Looking pissed and pleased at the same time. "Why is everyone picking on the girl?" Kyra ask. "Cause we can." Julian boast. I just laugh. Tuck gets up walks to her and slowly lifts her cut off shirt exposing her black laced bra and big sexy as hell tits. I think I'm drooling and all of us are staring. Tuck goes back to his seat but keeps her shirt. Back to Julian "truth or dare Krya?" "Dare" she giggles the girl is wasted. "Go set on Tucks lap facing us." Huh? She does as he says but Tuck doesn't look happy. I laugh this is getting good. "Truth or dare Jax?" Kyra ask "dare" of course. "I dare you to kiss Julian." Wtf? I get up and peck him on his cheek. Kyra laughs "nope full kiss or no partying." Shit I've never kissed a man before. But if I'm gonna play might as well play on tilt. I get up and kiss Julian tongue and all. He grabs my head and makes me him kiss deeper. Not bad. Same as a woman. I'm slightly turned on. I break away look at Julian's dick and yep it's hard along with mine. Damn. "Ok Kyra wanna play those games? Tuck truth or dare?" "Dare" I dare you to finger Kyra." She looks shocked and her eyes goes wide. Yea play with me temptress I play hard. "If you don't Tuck no partying for you." He grunts. "Only if I have consent." He said. We look at Kyra waiting. "But you have a girlfriend." She says with innocence. Her big doe eyes all red and I know she high and probably horny too. "Not anymore" huffs Tuck "ok" she says. Hot damn! This just got real good. Tuck reaches his big hand around her waist and edges it down her pants. He starts moving his fingers and whispers in Kyras ear. I'm not close enough to hear it but I think he said you like it sugar? Kyra groans and starts moving her hips with his fingers and letting out little moans that have us all hard and jealous of fucking Tuck. It doesn't take long he has her gyrating and moaning all over his hand. His hand hand sneaks around and grabs her tit. Rubbing nonstop. She screams I'm cumming and let's loose with a hard rocked orgasm. Shuddering in is arms.

Damn I wish I was him. That dare just backfired on my ass. I look at the guys and their all fucking drooling. Tuck whispers in her ear again and she shakes. I guess from his deep voice. She raises her head and looks flushed and so fuckable. I resist the urge to go and jump her sexy little ass. Though it's hard. All of me is hard, fuck!

"Truth or dare Damon" says Julian how he can talk after that I don't know. "Dare" again "I dare you to take Kyras pants off." "Gladly" he says and jumps up in front of Kyra and Tuck. He unbuttoned her jeans and slowly takes them off. Leaving her in black lace bra and matching panties. Shit! He hands her a blunt and she greedily takes it. "Truth or dare Julian." Ask Damon. "Dare" still no truths. Damon gets on the couch takes a drag and says "I dare you to eat Kyra out." Her eyes go wide but smiles. Julian jumps up. Damn I think were all fucked! Julian walks slowly to Kyra and ask if it's ok? Yea says Kyra and man is she buzzing. He kneels in front of her slowly slides he panties off squats down and I set back and enjoy the show.

JULIAN

I must be dreaming. I'm high as fuck and I'm loving this. Dear sweet Kyra is naughty when she cuts loose. Now I'm gonna eat it up literally! I bend down in front of her. Her sweet pussy is on full on display. Pretty and pink and glistening from Tuck earlier. I lean over and lick her from asshole to clit. She taste like honey-dew and man I'm loving it. She wiggles under my onslaught and Tuck puts his hands on her waist to hold her still. I so appreciate it. I begin rotating my tongue on her dub and putting my fingers inside her. She's moaning and my dick is hard as hell. I bend my fingers and hit her gspot. She's losing control and I'm eating it up. I bite down on her nub gently and that sends her into over drive. I'm sucking and licking hard on her clit and then she cums. She yells my name and I keep going. I can't stop now. I don't want to stop. I've waiting six weeks for this and I'm gonna enjoy every luscious lick. Tuck starts groping her titties and pinching them. He whispers how he wants to put his cock so deep into her that she could taste his cum. Damn that even turns me on! I keep licking back and forth lavishing up every last drop of her as she cums again, all over my face and all in mouth. She taste so damn good. I want more. I need more. I stand up and pull out my rock hard cock. Stroking it right in front of her. She watches me with lust in her eyes. She reaches out and touches my head and I'm come undone I squirt semen all over her beautiful tits and stomach. I couldn't control myself but damn who could blame me. She rubs it on her stomach and brings her finger to her mouth and licks my cum into it. I think I love this woman. "Fuck that was hot!" Claims Jax damn right it was hot. This woman's going to be the death of me.

She jumps up runs to the bathroom. Did we upset her? Damn is she pissed? I go after her. I knock on the door a few times she opens it and looks up at me with her big smile. She takes my hand and drags me to her bedroom. Oh boy. I'm in deep. She climbs on the bed spreads her legs and starts fingering herself. I'm standing there with my dick on hard again wondering what to do.

"Finish the job Julian." I don't waste a second. I jump on her and slide between her legs. I start playing with her clit all over again she's so wet and I'm so ready.

"You sure cookie?" Please say yes. I'm dying to get in between her folds. "Yes, please" that's all it takes. I slide my cock on her pussy about to enter. But I hesitate. "We need a condemn cookie" she reaches over opens a drawer and grabs one out. She opens it and slowly rolls it down on my cock. Sexy as fuck. I groan roll back on top of her. I'm about to enter "it may hurt but just for a bit ok?" She nods. With a smile. I place my cock between her folds and enter slowly. I don't want to hurt her but I'm about to loose my control. I push in and break the her hymen. Damn , I still. Letting her adjust to me in her. She's starts rotating her hips and I let loose. Unable to control it any longer. I pound into her hard over and over. I rub her clit while I pounding her relentlessly and grabbing her ass. I entered heaven. She's like gold. I struck gold and I feel rich. So tight. So sweet. So fucking hot. So desirable.

She wraps her legs around me I get on my knees and grind hard into her. I lean over sucking on her breast and biting down. I ease my way up to her neck and suck down hard leaving a mark or two on her. All the while I'm playing with her clit and grinding on her. I go back to breast licking and sucking and enjoying every nibble. She groans and goes wild. "That's it baby. You like my cock pounding into your pussy don't you?" I go harder. She's closes her eyes moaning loudly. "Look at me baby, I want you to look at me when I make you cum. Scream my mother fucking name!" I keep pounding and pounding not giving her second to think. I leaned down about to reach my edge. She grabs my back and just as she cums she screams my name "Juliaaaan" and scratches down my back. A mix of pleasure and pain and I fucking love it. I squirt out fast and hard loosing air and control.

I keep going. Not letting up. Wanting and craving more. I spasm again the condemn is beyond full. She's panting and flushed when I look at her. "You ok?" She answers with one word.

"More" "Damn baby"

I'm done for and I'm falling hard for her. I slip on another condemn. We go another round. Fucking hard and no relenting. Over and over and over I grind into her. I flip her over, adjust myself back into her and bounce on into her super hard. I keep going not wanting to let up. I grab her nub and squeeze hard rotating it side to side. I bring me hand over her ass and put my finger in her asshole. Pumping in and out. She's shaking and screaming and I release in her again. Spent and exhausted and I'm still rock hard. How does she keep me so hard? I relent. I pull off the condemn and head to the bathroom. I come back with a wet towel and clean her. Throwing the towel in a hamper I jump back on the bed. I roll to the side and bring her over to me and kiss her forehead. The bedroom door squeaks open slowly and Jax peeks his head in. With a big ass smile.

"Guess the games over huh?" I laugh throw a pillow at him and as he leaves I swore he said lucky bastard.

We drift off to sleep.

———————————————————————————

The next morning I'm laying there watching her sleep on my chest. She's so damn beautiful. I can't get enough. She chose me. I can't believe she chose me to be her first. Out of all the men here. I'm the lucky one. I know she was high and drunk last night and I'm praying she has no regrets. I don't think I could live with myself if she does. Sure I've had plenty of women. But none like her. She gave me a gift and I plan to treasure it and her. I can see spending the rest of my life with her. But would she ever want to be with me? A stripper? A playboy? One who has never been faithful? I would for her. Only her. My cookie. My dream.

She stirs awake. I'm nervous like school boy. Hoping she doesn't regret it. Hoping that she still wants me.

"Morning" she breathes out. Here it goes. I'm on edge. "Mmorning" I stutter out. Geez what's wrong with me? "How did you sleep?" Holding my breath and praying. "Wonderfully" she looks at me her hair all in a mess but looking adorable and sweet.

"Do you? Do you regret last night?" She ask me. What? Never. How could I? I found heaven and I'm not letting it go. "Not in the least" I roll on top of her. She giggles. Yea I found my heaven alright. I kiss her. Deep and hard. She wiggles under me. I need to get under in control. I know she has to be sore.

"Come on. Let's go eat." She shakes her head. "I need a shower first. I'll meet you in there." She gets out of bed and kisses me headed for the shower. I walk into the kitchen the guys are already there. Tuck is cooking and Damon and Jax are on the stools. They look up at me and smile. Ok here we go. I'm ready for it. Their just jealous it wasn't them. Fuckers.

"So how was it?" Of course it's Jax that ask. Tucks turns around placing food in the plates. His eyebrows are raised wanting to hear the answer.

"It was heaven, plain and simple heaven" and that's I'm going to indulge to these assholes. "I bet, you lucky shit!" Coming from Damon, I'm surprised didn't think he was interested in her. I just smile sit down and start to eat. Im ravenous. "So you think she's open to just more than one?" Ask Tuck. Surprised again. Now he seems interested also. Im confused. But hey to each his own. I know how ravishing she is.

"You have to ask her" "Ask me what?" Said Kyra as she enters the kitchen in very short demon shorts a crop top and her hair still wet. Fucking looking like a goddess.

"If your into more than just one?" States Damon and looks at her expectantly. She looks confused so I explain. "More than just me.

More than just one guy. Like a poly relationship." Her beautiful eyes go wide.

This should be very interesting.

TUCK

She's staring at us like we lost our damn mind. Maybe we have. I don't know if I can do this. I'm possessive and yea I'm a jealous mother fucker. I don't think I can share her. I would want her just for me and me alone. I can't fathom why these guys would even want to share her in the first place. To know that another man is touching what's mine. Fucking what's mine. Loving what's mine. I couldn't deal with that.

Wait...love? Nah that even in the equation. There's no way I will allow myself to love her. I won't and can't have feelings for her. I know In my gut that Candance is with Chuck. It's what she's always wanted. Not me. I was a game to her. A ploy.

I should of just let her go a long time ago. But I couldn't. Blame it on me being selfish. Wanting to be the one to win or whatever but I just held on. Like a damn fool. So no, I couldn't love her. I will not give her my heart. I will not give anyone my heart. Never again.

"Are you crazy? Why...why...how would that even work?" She's all flustered and it's kind of cute. The shock on her face is comical.

"I don't think that is a good idea. I mean, come on. First,how would it work? Second, what about jealousy or loyalty? I mean I don't want to be the cause of either of you, fighting or getting mad at each other and Julian how do you even know if the others even want me? Or would go along with this? It's...it's insane!" She looks at us all and storms out the house.

"Well that went well," Jax exclaims "could of went a lot better. Now how do we convince her?" He puts his plate in the sink with a sigh rubbing his hand down his face. He really likes her. He's been on her since day one. I just don't get it.

"I don't know, but I do know that my feelings for her are not going to change, even if she agrees or not. I'm still going to find a way into her life. I will fight for her. She....she means a lot me." At Julian's announcement we all looked a bit shocked. Does he love her? I mean it's too soon. Right? How can he have feelings for her, this soon? I've heard about love at first sight but I have yet to know anyone who's experienced it. I know he slept with her, but love her?

"Do you love her, Julian?" I just don't get it. "Yea you know what, I do. I love her. I know it may seem to soon or whatever, but she's a stunning, beautiful, and thoughtful woman who has swept me off my feet. So yea I lover her." Wow ok then. I'm confused.

"Then how can you share her? I know if I loved her, I damn sure wouldn't want to share her! That's not love. That's just lust. Plain and simple brother." He jumps up off the stool mad as hell. Looks me dead in the eye. I've never seen him so mad.

"DONT JUDGE ME! If I have just a minuscule amount of love from her then that's enough for me. I don't do jealousy! I just love," he calms a bit sits back down. "besides I want her happy and if that's what makes her happy, then I'll do it! ITS NOT LUST!" Everybody goes quite. I'm looking at this fool like he has lost his damn mind. He's gone off the deep end.

"What the hell, Julian?" "Love? LOVE? You've got to be kidding me? You know damn well if you loved her you couldn't share her! Be a man! Does she even love you? Don't you care that she'll have other guys dicks in her! Fucking her? Making her scream their name and not yours?!" Catching my breath I look at him and in all my anger I said the words I will forever regret.

"All you want to do is turn her into your damn whore! Making her cum on other guys dicks why you watch and it breaks your heart that it's not you! She would be nothing but a cunt ass slut!!" "Is that what you want? For her to get you in her grasp and laugh behind your back, cause she's getting away with fucking all your friends! Loving how she's made a damn fool of you?! I will never share a stinking ass cunt!!" I take a breath I'm angry so angry. How could he fall for this? "You want to play her willing victim? You want be her pussy?! Why? Why would you fall for that? Why would you fall for a fucking easy lay, that would spread her legs for anybody?!" I hear a gasp and know I just fucked up. I turn and see Kyra in the doorway. Knowing she heard everything. Tears streaming down her   face. I could kick myself. I turn away from her not being able to look her in the eye. When I see a fist flying right at me. Knocks me me on my ass. Damn! I deserved that. But shit it hurts. I jump up to fight Julian but it's not him that slammed me. It's Damon. Wtf?

"You ever say another word like that about her and I'll fucking kill you! You hear me Tuck. One. Fucking. Word!" I didn't expect that. "Just leave! Get the fuck out! NOW!!" I rub my jaw and look around. Julian looks heartbroken. Jax is holding Kyra now while she cries and Damon's facing me breathing heavy ready for a face off. Pissed as hell.

I turn on my heel and leave outside. I'm pissed at them, but now I'm pissed at myself more. Why did I say anything? Why do I even care? Let them share her. It's none of my damn business. I won't have anything to do with it. I don't want her. Don't need her. Don't care.

Then why is bothering me so bad?

I hear footsteps behind me I turn and see Jax. Solemn expression on his face. I really don't feel like talking right now. I start to walk off then he speaks. Sighing beforehand I brace myself for the speech. I turn to him.

"You made her cry dude. She's been with one man. How does that make her a slut? A whore? She didn't even agree to it and just because Julian claims he loves her. You fly off like damn jackass and made her cry! Does it make you feel better,Tuck?"He coughs. I'm getting pissed again. I walk up to him about to lash out but holds up his hands.

"No Tuck, you're lying to yourself. You like her. Deep down you know that. You feel that. You do or you wouldn't have gotten so damn upset." He points his finger at me "It bothers you and you know it! You want her just as much as we do but you're a coward not to admit it. She's gotten under your skin and it's getting to you." Letting out a sigh he continues "Look Tuck I understand you more than you know. Yea you don't want to share. You don't think you can share her. But if you don't get your head out of ass you're going to missing out on the best thing of your life." And with that he walks off.

No. I don't agree. The best thing would be a honest faithful woman. Who just wanted me and no one else. Not someone I had to share. To me that isn't normal. It's ridiculous.

I stay outside till the sun starts going down. Exasperated I head back in. This day has been shit. My jaw hurts. I'm tired. I need a shower and bed.

As I walk into the open area I see all of them on the couch watching a movie. Looks like Halloween the first one. They have it way up loud. Kyra turns to me "dinners on the island, if your hungry." And turns around to continue to watch the movie.

I just walk off headed for a shower and then bed. Not caring to eat. On my way I hear Damon say don't worry about spitfire, we got you.

Yea they do. But she will never have me. That's for damn sure.

Kyra

Fuck

I'm sitting here on the couch with the guys. I've been crying all day. Now my shock and sadness has turned to anger. How dare he?! I've only slept with Julian that doesn't make me slut! Yes I was high and a bit drunk but I don't regret it. I'm 21, I was virgin! How does that make me a slut? Besides I would never hurt the guys. Not the way Tuck thinks anyway. I couldn't do that. I know what that pain feels like. It hurts. It tears you apart and leaves your soul to bleed. Destroys you from the inside out.

When I aged out of the system and had to fend for myself, I ended up trusting someone that I shouldn't have. Devon was loving and caring at first. He said all the right things. Made me feel special and loved. Little did I know what a creep he was. The entire time I was with him, he had another girlfriend. Luckily I never slept with the asshole.

We were only together for three months but it hurt non the less. I wish I knew what a jerk he was though. I left him high and dry and never looked back. I stand on my own. I'm not gonna let anyone use me or me them. I not made that way. I shuffle in my seat.

"You ok cookie?" Julian has been worrying over me since it happened. He's been so sweet. Even cooked for us. I heard him tell Tuck he loves me. I think I'm falling for him also but I don't dare say anything. I said it once before and I'm scared to say it again. I grab his hand and a fake a smile.

"Yes, I'll be ok," I fidget in my seat and look at the others they are just as worried. It bothers me that this effects them so much also. "He really didn't mean it. He doesn't know me. It's just the circumstances we are in. Nothing more. I'm fine." I really smile then. I'm not going to let Tuck get to me. I'm stronger than that and I truly think it's because of the stress we're all under. I can't really blame him but he didn't have to resort to saying all those awful things about me.

Then out of the blue there's a loud bang outside. A large flash of light is seen outside the window. We all jump and get up to run out. Tuck comes out of his room and runs along with us. We all go to the side of house and see a big burnt spot on the ground. Smoke still coming out of circle. It smells of vanilla. For some strange reason. We hear a coughing and we all turn to the sound. There's a man walking toward us. He's tall with broad shoulders. His black hair hangs just below shoulders. He's dressed in a blue sweatsuit. As he gets closer I see his eyes. They're as blue as the sea. He's handsome and well built. He clears his throat. Turns his eyes on each of us. I get a bad vibe from him. He's not like the others. I can just feel it for some reason. He seems cold and distrustful.

"Sorry folks, didn't mean to frighten you. Uhm may I ask where am I and who you are?" His voice is deep. Sends shivers down my spine. How did he get here? Something doesn't seem right. I look at the guys and seem as shocked as me.

"First, who the hell are you?" Tuck ask still in his bad mood I see. Showing this stranger his anger. Though I really can't blame him at this point.

"I'm Tim Myers. I'm a bit confused as to how I'm here. I was on my to my library. I opened the door and suddenly it's like I'm pulled from my home and end up here. Wherever here is." As he looks around then turns back to us. He coughs again then comes closer. I step back a bit scared of the newcomer. He sees this and laughs. "I'm not gonna to hurt you honey, I mean you no harm." Then laughs again. He may not, but I don't know him and I don't trust easy.

Julian steps up, ever the peace maker and reaches out for the man to shake his hand. "I'm Julian, this is Damon, Tuck, Jax, and she's Kyra." As he points to each of us. The man doesn't shake his hand.

Very rude if you ask me. "Nice to meet you all. Can someone please explain to me how I got here and where exactly is here?" He raises his eyebrow and looks at us all. We hesitate to answer. Not knowing if we can trust him or not.

"That will take a bit longer. So why don't you tell us why we should trust you? You just pop in here out of nowhere and you expect us to believe that you have no idea how you got here?" Thank you Tuck. My thoughts exactly. He looks surprised at Tucks tone. Ha if you knew him you wouldn't be surprised at all. He is the beast after all. I silently laugh. Tuck is a force to be reckoned with. At this moment I'm sort of proud of him.

"I'm sorry I can't answer that because I have no idea. How did you get here? Yet I ask again where is here?" I don't believe him. I don't know why but I just don't. We all came here together, he shows up alone and he really doesn't looked worry at all. Not like we were. Maybe he's the one that sent us here? Maybe he's responsible for all this? I don't know but I'm weary.

"Let's just go inside and talk this out. We will explain how we got here and you will tell us Everything you know, ok?" Jax said. Who knew he had a level head. We all go back in the house. All the men are up front and I stay near the back. We go into the living room. They all sit down i stay standing behind them. I don't dare turn my back on him.

Julian begins telling him how we all got here. All the details of the last six weeks. Leaving out the sexual parts. Thank God. I would be horrified. He listens closely, never interrupting. Shaking his head as if deep in thought. Then he turns to me. I step back as his eyes penetrate me.

"You're the only female here? Interesting. I wonder why?" I don't care why. I just want him to stop looking at me. Damon sees that I feel uneasy and gets up to come over to me. He walks behind me and puts his arms around my waist in a hug. He whispers and ask if I'm ok? I just shake my head. Not wanting to voice my reactions.

He stays behind me as Tim watches us both closely. Eyeing me up and down. I get a chill and feel it in bones. Damon grips me tighter and ask if I want to go outside. I jump at the chance. Turning and bolting right out the door as he follows. He stops as reach the pool. The moonlight is casting off the water.

"What's wrong? You've been acting strange since he showed up. Talk me spitfire." He seems frustrated. I take a deep breath. Looking back to see if anyone can hear.

"I don't Damon. He seems fishy to me. He gives me the chills. I don't trust him." I whisper to him. Damon grabs my chin and turns me to him. Looking me in the eyes. "It's ok I will not let anyone hurt you. Do you trust Me spitfire?" I nod my head "then believe me when I tell you that I will not let anything happen to you. I will kill any mother fucker that hurts you. Do you understand?" I nod my head again. I'm at a loss for words. He wraps me in his arms and hugs me. He turns my head to a different angle. To where I'm facing him. Then he kisses me.

I'm shocked at first. His tongue dives into my mouth and feels so good. I wrap my arms around his neck and pull him closer. He kisses like a God. I moan as he takes his hand and grabs for ass, squeezing and groping. I'm lost in his touch. It's electrifying. Torturing me in the sweetest way. We hear someone clear their throat and jump apart. Slightly embarrassed for being caught I turn my head. Damon just smiles. Oh boy I love that smile. A devil with a boyish charm. I turn back and look to the intruder.

"So sorry to interrupt your a...make out session. But I have a few more questions, if you don't mind," said Tim as he smirks and looks away. Damon kisses me on my forehead and walks back in passing Tim. He then looks at me "I see your already taken, mores the pity. I for one think you can better. But that's just me." He laughs as he walks off. I look at his retreating back in disgust.

There's no way I'm trusting this guy now. It's bad enough that I have to deal with Tuck and his attitude, now I have to deal with a demon also. Men are rather confusing. I huff. I walk back in. Everybody is In Their same positions. I still stand back. To and keep listening. You can learn more when your quiet and nobody notices you. Unfortunately Tim does notice. A little too much. If I might add. He turns to me and winks. The nerve of this guy. I decide to go sit on Julian's lap. Since he's in the far chair. Tim watches and raises his eyebrows as Julian wraps me in his arms pulling back to him. Gripping me fighting and caressing my stomach.

"Cozy are we?" Tim ask I roll my eyes. This jackass is on my nerves! "More than you know," I say as I turn to Julian and out of spite kiss him. I don't know what I was trying to prove. But it felt good and I wanted to put Tim in his place. I turn my attention back to him "Now what questions do have?" I say with a smirk of my own. I look over at Tuck and I see he is gnawing his jaw. I don't care. Let him stew. I look at Damon and Jax and their both smiling. Then I look at Tim, wish I didn't though, he has lust filled eyes and evil grin. Tuck notices also he looks more upset now. But why would he even care? He's made his feelings clear. I'm done with all this. After today my nerves are on edge.

"I'm going to bed, I've enough for tonight. Can someone please show Tim to a room," I turn to Jax "care to join me?" I have no idea what's gotten into me but I like it. I feel empowered and a little devious. "Hell yea!!" Jax jumps up and picks me up bridal style. I just laugh at his antics. He turns and says night boys. Then We head to my to my room. He looks at me with a giant smile and he's hot as hell. With his tattoos and lip ring. His hot as sin body and a gleam in his eye, I think to myself,

What have I gotten myself into?

———————————————————————-Thank you to all those who are taking to time to read my first story. It truly means a lot to me. I'm an avid reader and just thought I'd give it a shot. I hope you like it. Thanks again pretties.

Damon

Watching as Kyra and Jax go to her room, I'm consumed with jealousy and arousal. He's about to have a dream come true and I'm stuck here with Tim and the guys. I don't trust Tim. Kyra is scared of him and for whatever reason I trust her instincts. He seems devious and calculating. My nerves are on edge and I'm tired of listening to his prattle.

"Have you tried to find away back home? Look for an explanation? There has to be a reason why we all ended up in this desolate place," he ask, but sense no unease from him. It's like he already knows the answer. "Not to sound rude, but it seems as you have accepted your fate, does the girl have to something to do with why you all are not in a rush to leave?" That does it. I'm done with this fucker. I grunt and get up about to head to room. I look back at the guys and just shake my head. Headed to my destination I hear moans coming from Kyras room.

I hesitate. I want to enter and view what treasure I'm going to receive in my future.i don't want to seem like perv. Fuck this, I open the door and enter her room. Kyra is sprawled out on the bed, naked. Legs opened wide. Jax is down between her legs eating her out. Neither notices my entry. Kyra is grasping the sheets and moaning. She looks delectable. In the throws of passion.

I moan out from my lust. Jax stops and looks up and smiles. Her nectar is all over his face. He's enjoying himself immensely. Kyra looks at me and her eyes are filled with desire. She seems ok with me being here. So I'm going to enjoy the show.

"Continue" as I go to sit on the chair in the corner. Jax doesn't hesitate and lowers head back to his treat. Kyra progresses with her moaning. She's gyrating her hips as he goes. I pull out my cock that's standing at full attention. Gripping it in my hand and stroking it slowly. I want to get involved but I'm not ready yet. So instead I'll orchestrate.

"Jax, suck her tits!" He looks at me and climbs upward and starts sucking her globes. Her big and round beautiful breast. I continue my ministrations. "Finger her!" I grunt out and Jax drops his hands to her mound as I try to hold back fulfillment. Kyras is groaning and wanting more. I oblige. "Jax, fuck her!" He looks at me with adulation. He reaches for the condemn they have laid out and puts it on. He starts to enter her. "Go slow!" I grunt out. He goes extremely slow as he enters her. This torture is sweet but maddening. As he's slowly pumping into her I pick up my speed on my aching cock. Picturing her soft lips surrounding it. Wishing I was brave enough to join. "Go faster," I demand and Jax starts slamming into her hard. Kyras breast and bouncing and her moans are coming closer and more erratic. "Stop! Flip her over," he does as he's told. Places Kyra on all four, her ass in the air. I see her cum glistening on her pussy. I'm about to lose it so slow down stroking myself. It's better than torture at this point. "Fuck her hard and place your fingers on her clit!" Again he obeys. He picks up speed and his hands are going wild. Rubbing her nub. "Put your finger in her ass," he does Krya clenches at the intrusion. Jax hesitates. Relax spitfire, take it all in, you will enjoy it." As she relaxes Jax places one finger in her hole. I tell Jax to add an additional finger. He does going back and forth and increasing his speed. He's pumping in her and fingering her ass hard. She's spiraling with fulfillment. I'm about to come undone. "Flip her over," he pulls out and tosses her on her back. He enters her again and starts humping her nonstop. Kyra wraps her legs around his waist. I can tell she's almost there. So am I. I speed up my ejaculation. Bracing myself for my fulfillment and theirs. Cum! Now!" And all three of us do. Kyra screams Jax name. Jax screams Kyras name and I release all over myself. Content and happy.

I jump up and go to the bathroom cleaning myself. I get a towel,wet it, and go back to clean Krya. She's spread eagle on the bed and I take the towel and clean her. She moans when I do. I laugh. "Get under the cover spitfire," she does contentment all over her face. I place the cover over her. Jax is disposing of the condemn, then he crawls in beside her. Spooning her. I reach down and push her hair to side and kiss her cheek. "Good girl, you did really well." She sighs and I look at Jax "night guy." And I leave the room, closing the door behind me. It was exhilarating and I can't wait to fuck her. I turn to look at the gentleman in the living room. Their all looking me, Julian is smiling. Happy no doubt that we experienced what he has. Not knowing that I still haven't gone all the way with her. Tuck looks pissed. Well that's on him. He needs to grow a pair and deal with it. Tim on the other hand looks piqued and way to interested. I go to stand in front of them waiting for whatever comments they want to throw my way.

"Seems I've landed in a place that entices me. Do you think she will have me also?" Tim ask, wtf? Is he serious?

"I don't think it works that way," Tuck answers. Tim looks at Tuck raises his eyebrows and stands. "Well maybe I'll just have to take it without having to say pretty please." He smirks. Wanting a reaction. Boy does he get one. Tuck jumps out of his seat and dives for Tim. Knocking him and the couch over simultaneously. He lands on top of Tim and starts pounding him in the face. Kyra and Jax emerge from the bedroom, their confused and running over to to Tuck. Julian and I jump over to Tuck and Tim and try to pull Tuck off of Tim before Kyra can get closer. We pull him off. I'm holding him.

Which is hard cause this guy is humongous and mad as hell. Julian rights the couch and we leave Tim on the floor. He deserves it. What an asshole. Threatening rape! I'll kill the bastard. Tuck shakes me off and sits on the couch. "First aid kit!" Julian yells at Jax, he takes off to retrieve it. Kyra goes over to Tuck and squats in front of him. "Throw this asshole in a room! We will deal with him later!" I yell at Julian, he picks him up and goes in search for a room. I'm pissed as hell. Jax returns with the kit and hands it to Kyra. She opens it and starts doctoring Tucks hand. It's busted and bleeding. Has to hurt.

"What happened?" Jax ask, I start to answer him but Tuck speaks up "He threatened to rape Kyra!" Kyra gasps and looks terrified. Now I'm more than pissed seeing the fear in her eyes. "But why? I don't understand?" States Kyra. Yea me either babe.

I look at Jax and he's steaming. "I'll fucking kill him! I'll kill that son of bitch! He goes anywhere near her and he's a dead man! We have to do something!" My sentiments exactly. Julian enters the room. "I threw him in the room next yours Damon. He's out cold. Any idea on what to do with him?" Yea one. I grab my switchblade from my pocket. Open it. "Yea we kill him. Now." I look at all them. Jax is in agreement. Julian looks shocked. The pussy. Tuck has no reaction. He's staring at Kyra and she is motionless.

"We can't just kill him! He threatened yes, but he it's not he did it! We just can't kill someone from just stating what they plan to do! That's insane!" As usual, Julian is over reacting. I don't see the problem. I've killed before it would be easy to kill this mother fucker. I'd do it with no qualms.

"You ok sugar?" Tuck ask Kyra as he's rubbing his finger down her face. She blinks and looks at Tuck and nods her head but there's tears in her eyes. She finishes her ministrations on Tucks hand. Closes the kit and begins to stand. Tuck grabs her and places her on his lap. Her short silk robe slides up as she sits across his lap. He leans in and places his face on her shoulder and sniffs her. He sniffed her! What the?

She wraps her arms around his neck and cries. My spitfire is crying! That done it! "Im going to kill him!" I turn to head to his room. Julian stops me by grabbing my arm. "Don't touch me!" He drops his hand. "We can't kill him. We can lock him up? Put a guard on him? But we can't kill him Damon!" Im exasperated. I want to kill him. I need to kill him!

"No" it's a whisper but we heard it. "No, we can't kill him. It was all talk. Unless he actually does something, then we can. Until then, well we just can't. It's inhuman." Kyra says. I don't agree. Why wait till he does something!? That's asking for trouble.

I stay quiet. I will bode my time. Sneak into his room and take him out. No matter how much they protest. Im not willing to take the chance with my spitfire. No one is going hurt her. I don't know where all this possessiveness comes from I just know I need to protect her. My woman. My heart.

Damn! My heart! Wait!

I love her!

Omg! I love her. Me? I don't do love! I kill! I hurt! I'm a monster! How can a monster love? It's unheard of. I don't understand. My emotions are on high. How did this happen? No one has effectively wormed their way into my heart like she has. My woman. My spitfire. Jesus!!

"Kyra...i uh..." I'm at a lost. "I'll take care of him!" How do I tell her? How do I show her how much she means to me? I've never experienced this before. It's a new emotion for me. I'm fucking clueless! I look at her and her face is full of worry. I want to take that away. I want her to be happy again. I'll kill him for her. All for her. I have too, it's the one way I can show her I care. Right? Hell I'm more confused than ever.

"Sugar, I want someone around you at all times. You go nowhere without one of us, understand? And you don't sleep alone. One of us sleeps with you. I'm serious Kyra, at all times!" Tuck tells her and I look at him. He has pure devotion all over his face and he's rubbing her back while he holds on to her. Not wanting to let go.

He loves her! The asshole loves her! That's why he's fighting so hard? Unbelievable! Well that's three that's in love with her. I don't know about Jax. He acts as if he does but I could be fooled. Tuck stands holding Kyra in his arm bridal style. He looks at us "I'll take first shift. Somebody might want to guard his door. I'll watch her tonight." And they go to his room.

"Well I'll be damned! Did you see that?" I ask still entranced.

"He loves her. The prick loves her!" Says Jax. My thoughts exactly.

Boy are we fucked!

———————————————————————

Thank you for reading. Pls vote or comment. Till next pretties!

TIM

I come awake with pain. My face is on fire. These fools have no idea the hurt I will bestow upon them! The room is aglow with moonlight spilling into the room. Damon sets in the corner on an old recliner I see the gleam of a switchblade resting on his lap.

The idiot! I wave my my hand and put him into a deep slumber. They have no idea who they are messing with. I Dakur an evil grand wizard of the higher power has come out to play. I sensed their heartbeats in my own realm. None suppose to be here. They have no idea they were casted here by a witch. What witch and of what realm I do not know. It makes no consequence to me. I've come to deviate and destroy.

I raise my hand to heal my face. I stagger to the bathroom. Cast a light and look at my reflection in the dirty mirror. I see the evil glint in my eyes and my devilish smirk. Yes I'm evil and I revel in it, I enjoy the hunt. The prey. The fear. With a female here, my heart beats with elation. I will torment and torture her very soul. Rip apart her innocence. Have my diabolical way with her, all while the others watch. I cannot wait.

I leave the bathroom and step out of the bedroom into the hall. Damon won't wake for a very long time. That diminishes my fun. I ponder upon it and decide to return later. I'll return the following night. Let them search for me and wonder of my whereabouts. Then come back, in the night like a thief to still their very souls, to have my fill of fun and pain.

I snapped my fingers and return to my realm.

————————————————————————————- Kyra

"Tuck, please put me down." As we enter his room. I'm surprised at how my beast is acting lately. Something has changed in him. I'm starting to worry. "I'm ok, please." He sets me on my feet but doesn't let me go. I look at him, he's so handsome, so manly, and so stunning. He takes my damn breath away. He grunts and turns around. He removes his shirt and the sight is so damn mesmerizing. His toned back. His rippled muscles. My hot pocket is going crazy. I feel tingles in my spine. I'm fucking spellbound.

"Get into bed, I'll sleep on the sofa." As he grabs a pillow and blanket from the corner of the room. Laying them on the small sofa in his room. The sofa is worn and outdated a dingy brown color. It looks very uncomfortable. I suddenly feel guilty for putting him out. "It's ok, Tuck I'll sleep on the sofa. You take the bed. It's yours after all." I half laugh and turn my head away.

"I'm fine, sleep," I huff out. Men! Why does it have to be so hard? "No Tuck either you sleep in your own bed or I'll return to my room. This is ridiculous." He turns to look at me. He seems more upset. I step back. He sighs and starts coming my way. He stops in directly in front me. Bends down and picks me up. I let out a yelp. He throws me on the bed and pulls the cover over me. "I said sleep!" He turns and walks back to the dingy sofa. Fine! I remove my robe and lay down with a giant huff.

I will never understand Tuck. He's so damn complicated and annoying. One second he hates me the next he's nice to me. It's not like I chose to be in this situation. Stranded with four men. Now five. I shiver as I think of Tim. His threat is omnipresent. He scares me to no end. I hope he leaves. Somehow. I wish we all could leave.

"Tuck?" He grunts, like the sourly beast he is "Do you ever think we will return back home? I mean, it's not like I'm missing much there, but I do miss it. Don't you?" I can barely see him but he rolls onto his back and raises his hand behind his head. "Maybe,I don't know and no the only thing I miss is my brother." His brother. I can only imagine how much he that he does miss him.

"Tell me about him, please," I add the please, I don't want Tuck upset at me, for some reason. I grow tired of his anger all time. "He's my twin. We were are inseparable. Till Casandra came along. He's a firefighter. Loves his job. He was born for it. I guess that's why I became a cop. Different ends of the spectrum." He turns on his side "he is a better man than me. He's always happy and helps anyone in need. Never complains. He was parents favorite. I can't blame them. He's my favorite also." He says with sadness. Was? I guess his parents are gone? I would love to have a family. Any family. A brother would be nice. Someone to protect and look after me. Someone to love.

"I'm sorry Tuck. I wish I could send you home. I'm sure he's missing you too," he rolls back over onto his back.

"Yea, maybe. I think he's with Casandra now. If she has her way he is. She's undoubtedly with him that's for damn sure." I wish I could hug him. Take away his pain. But I don't dare. Her may bite off my fucking head. "Why did you stay with her? If she wants your brother so bad and why would he be with her? She doesn't seem nice at all?" He laughs

"She's not, it was more of a competition thing. Like, I got her she's mine and not yours type of thing, I don't know, seems silly now. And as for Chuck he would only want her to show me that he won. It's always been a competition between us. It use to be fun.

Not anymore." That's strange, but I've never had a sibling so I don't understand the dynamic. I set up to look at him.

"Tuck, you shouldn't have to compete for love. It should come gradually or at first sight. Winning isn't always important." He laughs. But I'm being serious. I don't think it's funny. I lay back down in a huff. Cross my arms. Trying to talk to this man is so damn infuriating!

"I see that now, sugar, just wish I saw it before. I wasted years competing with him. I just want a normal relationship with him now. What about you? Is there no one you miss?" Not a single person. I've always been lonely. One creep of a boyfriend and no friends. No family. No one. "No, there's no one. Absolutely no one."

He stays quiet. Too quiet. I look over and he hasn't moved. Please don't feel sorry me. I don't want your pity. I need no one's pity. I'm fine on my own. Always have been. But I'm really not on my own anymore am I? I have Julian. He loves me. I love him. Though I don't know if it will be the same for him if we make it back home. That's a scary thought. I don't want to lose him.

"Tuck?" He doesn't answer, is he asleep? "Tuck?" He grunts. "Yes" I don't know if I should ask him. I don't want to upset him. "Yes" he says a bit louder. "Do you think.....uhm.....do think Julian really loves me?" I know it's dumb. How would he truly know. But I want some sort of confirmation.

"Yes sugar I do," I picture him smiling "He is dumbstruck with love. So is Jax and Damon." I don't think so. At least they haven't said anything. No they don't love me. I feel flutters with them. I'm attracted to them both. I can't picture my life without them now. Is that love? My love for Julian is pure. I know I love him. Could I be in love with all three?Does Tuck care for me?

"Tuck?" "Yes sugar" I'm aggravating him. I can hear it in his tone. But I want to know. I need to know. "Do you care for me?" I don't dare say love. I know he doesn't. He's shown it more times than I can count. But I am his friend right? I care for him. I don't want to lose him either. He means a lot to me. They all do. Am I being selfish by not telling them all? Do I really care for them all? I think I do. I think I love them all. All of them. Oh no! That can't be, can it? Can I truly love them all? Yes, I think I do. I know I do.

"No Kyra, I don't care for you," well that broke my heart. But what else could I expect. He's shown me plenty of times. I irritate him. I confuse him. I'm not his friend. I feel tears come to my eyes. Why do I let him get to me!? It hurts. The rejection hurts more than I thought it would. I sniffle. I don't want him to know how it effects me. How his words hurt me. So I roll over and try to be quiet and pray for sleep.

"No Kyra, I don't care for you, I love you. I just don't know how to deal with that emotion when it comes to you. I just don't know how to........share!" He loves me? He loves me? I jump from the bed and run over to him. I crash on top of him and start kissing him.

I'm lost in his kiss. Our tongues clash and I feel sparks all over me. Then he pushes me away. I raise up and stare at him. Confused and I know it shows. "We can't do that Kyra! I said no before and I'm saying no now! I do not and will not share you! Now go to bed. Please." I get off of him and return to bed. I cover myself and roll over. I'm done. I can't deal with the back and forth anymore. It's literally breaking me into pieces.

"Ok Tuck, it's fine, I understand, but I'm done with the games. I can't take it anymore. It hurts to bad." With that I try to go to sleep.

"Kyra please I'm sorry. You have to understand." I don't answer him. What can I say. It's ok to keep ripping me apart. It's ok to toss my feelings around like they don't matter. I stay quiet. "Kyra?" silence. "Kyra?" I will not reply. I can't. My tears are falling and I'm speechless. "Kyra?" Nothing. "Fuck!!" He gets up and storms out.

I lay there with my thoughts and broken heart. I'm just not good enough. I will not give up Julian. Nor Jax or Damon. I love them. I don't need Tuck to make me fucking complete. I do love him also but I will have to love him from afar.

If he will let me.

————————————————Thank you for reading my
pretties.

TUCK

"**F**uck!"

I get up and leave the room. Slamming the door. I got to the living room. No one's there so I'll crash here. I can't deal with Kyras emotions right now! I'm worried about Tim and his threats.

I made her cry. I always make her cry. I can't seem to do a damn right, not when it comes to her. Now with Tims threat looming over our heads, I feel like I could explode at any moment. These are my thoughts I fall into a dreamless sleep.

————I wake up to a crash and Julian yelling. Shut up already, my damn head is pounding. "Shit, shut the fuck up! I'm trying to sleep!" Anger is boiling in me. Kyra,Tim, and now Julian's temper tantrum is enough to send anyone over the edge.

"Sorry Tuck, have you seen Damon?" He hurriedly ask, why would I have seen Damon? "I thought you were with Kyra? Why are you here on the couch?" I roll my head to look at him "Did you leave Kyra alone? What the hell! You dumb ass!" He takes off, I jump up, going to my room. I didn't think. Damn! I left her alone! I jump off the couch and run to my room. Nearly falling over at the loss of speed. I look in my room and see Julian holding Kyra, rocking her back and forth.

"Is she ok?" I bristle at his look. He's pissed. "Yea, no thanks to you. You were suppose to guard her Tuck, why would you leave her alone?" I don't have an answer for that. "Come on cookie, let's get ready for the day." She climbs off the bed. Looks at me when she gets besides me and exits the room.

"Great job Tuck, you moron!" He leaves the room. I sigh, I guess I am. I didn't think. I go shower, get dressed, in jeans and blue tee. I slip on my socks and boots and head for the kitchen. I go to the cabinet grab some aspirin and a water and turn to look at everyone. Jax is cooking eggs. Julian's pouring drinks. Kyras sitting on the stool with her head down. I swallow my aspirin and sit beside Kyra.

"Did you find Damon?" I ask Julian He blanches and takes off to look for him. A few seconds later, "GUYS COME HERE!" Julian yells. We head off down the hall. Me in front. Kyra behind me. Jax is still cooking. We entire Tims room. The beds empty and in the corner is Damon asleep. Jax enters a second later.

"You found him, wake him up," I tell Julian. "I've tried, he won't wake up!" Huh? "Shake him," "I've tried" Julian looks at me like I'm the crazy one. I walk over to Damon and shake him hard. He won't wake up. "Get me some water," Jax takes off to get it. I didn't realize how much of a heavy sleeper Damon was. Jax returns I take the water and throw on Damon. He doesn't stir. "What the hell?" He should of woke up. I look at everyone and their all confused too.

"Kiss him temptress, maybe he will wake up then," Jax snorts. Kyra slaps his arm. "Shit up goofball! This isn't a fairytale and I'm no princess." Ha she is to me, but that's beside the point. We can't seem to wake Damon. "Tickle him," states Julian, hell no! The dick would slice my throat open. "No way, he will kill me." Jax laughs. I look at Kyra.

"Sugar give a try, it couldn't hurt." I meant it as a joke but she bends over and kisses him on the lips. She raises up and looks at us. "See, not a princess." She says triumphantly. No but your a mother fucking Queen! I think to myself and laugh at my thought. Then Damon grunts. Holy shit! Maybe she is a princess. Ha, it worked. "See told ya!" Jax of course states.

Damon opens his eyes and looks around. "What's up?" As he rubs his eyes. "Dude Kyra had to kiss you to wake your dumbass up!" Claims Julian, Kyras blushing. Awe so cute.

"Why am I wet?" Grunts Damon, I look at Jax, he smiles and runs from the room. Pussy! "We couldn't wake you man, you're a damn heavy sleeper." I say stepping back as Damon puts away his blade and gets up.

"Where's Tim?" Huh? Forgot about the devil himself. We look around. "I've searched most the house looking for you," Julian says as he points to Damon "he's nowhere around." We all look at each quizzically. "Well he couldn't have gone far, this place isn't that big." As Damon leaves the room, we all exit and go back to the kitchen.

Kyra sets back on the stool as Jax puts food on our plates. Julian passes out the OJ and I guess Damon went off to change. We all set to eat and Damon returns dryer with a black shirts and pants. He sets next to Kyra and starts to eat.

"We need to find him. We can pair up in teams and search the town." States Damon while chewing his food. Damn dude close your mouth. "And don't leave Krya alone, no matter what." I look at Julian, feeling guilty. I look at Kyra she still has her head down. Barely eating. I did that. I made her feel that way. My gut is twisting.

"It was mistake ok! It won't happen again!" I yell out. Damon drops his fork and glares at me. So does Jax. "You left her alone?" Damon is seething. Jax is also. I fucked up I know that geez! "I'm sorry," I say it but I'm looking at Kyra not them. She raises her head looks at me and just drops her head again. Damn! I'm an idiot!

"Why? What happened? What was more important than staying with her, knowing Tim was right down the damn hall?!" Damon screams. I know I fucked up, but he has no right! "It's none of your damn business!" I scream at him. Kyra gets up, goes to her room and slams the door. I look at them all and they all look about ready to kill me. They love her and I put her life in danger just because I was mad. I am an idiot. They don't say a word though. Damon gets up and heads to Kyras room. He knocks and ask if he can come in. She lets him him. We hear the lock click. I'm feeling worse than ever. Guilts eating me up.

Julian and Jax just looks at me with disgust on their faces. Jax rolls his eyes and then they leave out the door. I guess to hunt for Tim. I'm here all alone, with my suffering and guilt. I clean the off the dishes and put them in dishwasher. Slamming the door. Rubbing my hand down my face. I take off to Kyras room to apologize and beg for her forgiveness.

I stand there debating on what to say. I have no idea. My feelings for her is complicated, to say the least. I love her there's no doubt in that.

But my anger got the best of me and I neglected her safety, like a damn fool. I got lucky that nothing happened to her. If something did, I probably couldn't live with myself.

I raise my hand to knock on the door but before I do, I stop. I hear moaning coming from her room. Damon and Kyra are making Lois's grunts and groans. Fuck! Now what do I do? I go to the open the door but forgot it was locked. I want to punch something or someone. I go to my room and crash on my bed.

Hearing her moans is agonizing. The walls are paper thin and I can hear everything. Her cries of passion are turning me on. I fight the urge, but I can't. Wishing beyond hope, that it was me and not Damon. I unbutton my jeans and release my cock. The pressure of how hard I am was suffocating. I her her moan and start rubbing my cock. Picturing her little hands on the base of it and her plump lips kissing it. Her looking into my eyes with heat and desire. Wanting to pleasure me, only me. I'm lost in my daydream of how magnificent it could be. Her moans are getting louder. Damon's grunting. She screams Yes!Yes! Yes! And I release my pleasure all over me. Exasperated and edgy. Shit! I go to clean up and change my jeans. I can't take this anymore. I need air. I exit the house to go look for Tim.

I want her. I crave her. I need her. But I just fucking can't have her. I know I'm an asshole. I want to give in. She's worth it I know. But I can't seem to do it. It's making crazy!

I storm off in search for the evil asshole that is tormenting my thoughts. It's better to think of him, than Kyra. It's like the lesser of two evils, so to speak. I spot Jax up ahead.

"Anything?" I ask he just looks at me and grunts. Then turns to start walking off. I grab his shoulder. "Look Jax, I fucked up! I'm sorry." He turns to me "don't apologize to me, apologize to her." He shakes my hand off. "Well I would but Damon is keeping her busy," I say with disgust. He laughs and gets in face.

"Jealousy is ugly Tuck! Grow the fuck up!" And storms off.

I'm left with my mouth agape and confusion written all over my face. Dudes younger than me and I should grow up? Hell yeah I'm jealous but grow up? Really?

I run my hand through my hair. I take off walking searching buildings. I bump into Julian. He screams and scares the shit out of me. "What the fuck Tuck! You scared the shit out of me!" I laugh, me too buddy. He goes to walk off. "Julian....I'm sorry," he looks at me. Basically he says the same thing as Jax said and then adds "Tuck, I just thought you were a better man." And walks away.

What. The. Actual. Fuck?

I'm at a loss. Am I really that bad? Have I been that bad? I think about it and realize yeah maybe I have. I've treated Kyra like shit. Pushed her away and keep breaking her heart. I am actually that bad. I'm the creeper! Realization hits me and I feel more guilty and ashamed than ever. I need to change this situation. I need to make things right.

I head off back to the house, ready to get on my damn knees if I have to and earn her forgiveness. I'm determined now and more at ease with my decision. I will be a better man. I may not sleep with her, but I will stand with her. If she will let me. If she can forgive me.

One can only hope.

——————————

Thank you for reading pretties. Comment and vote thanks.

Damon

"Can I come in?" I ask Kyra. I need to see if she's ok. She looked so upset. She opens the door and lets me in. I turn and lock it. She looks at me, she's sad, I'm gonna make her feel better or least try. That's my end game.

"You ok spitfire?" I ask and she nods her head. "Words baby," I grab her chin and make her look at me. "Yes" she whispers. I can't take her being sad or hurt. It breaks my heart. "Want me to make it better?" I ask as I lean down to her ear and whisper "I can, just say yes, baby!" As kiss her neck and lick down her throat. "Yes" she whispers again. I look at her and I'm a goner. So sweet and caring. But she has a hard determination. It's my turn.

"Strip," I tell her and back up to watch the show. She does as I ask and slowly takes off her robe. She reaches for her top "slowly, baby" she takes her top off very slow. She reaches for her bottoms and gracefully takes them off. She's standing there in her tan bra and panties. All lace and the bra has a little bow. I look over her. Up and down. A fucking goddess!

"Continue," my voice is straining, a bit and I'm starting to sweat. She removes them both and stands there in all her glory. The woman is titillating. Big breast. Bare pussy. Skin with a golden hue. Her hair is falling down her front. She's opening herself up and baring it all. All for me. "Get on the bed. Spread your legs, wide." She climbs on the bed. Opens her legs. I got to the end of the bed and stand, looking down at her. She is a sight. She watches me with a curious look. "It's okay baby, finger yourself!" I demand as I release my cock from my pants. Grabbing the base and stroking it. She takes her right hand and lowers it to her mound. Already wet and shiny. She opens her folds and places two fingers on her nub and begins to rub. I walk to the side of the bed as I continue to rub my cock. I stop and get undress. Grabbing a condom out of the drawer. "Put it on me!" She raises up and opens the packet and slowly guides it down my cock. "Lay down baby" I watch her then I climb on the bed.

I get between her legs and reach for her pussy as I suck on her tits. One then other. I tell her "you're so fucking beautiful. You drive me crazy." Circling her nipples and biting down gently. I want to go harder. Bite her all over, leave my marks. But I don't think she's ready for that, just yet. I'm rubbing her nub and fingering her hole. I bend my fingers and hit her gspot, going in and out. Faster and faster. I drop my hand and reach for asshole. I gently add one finger pumping in and out, then I Add another. I ease off her. I raise up on my knees. God she's enticing. "Roll over!" I command, and she rolls over, puts her ass in the air. I put my fingers back in her asshole. Take my other hand and use the cum to lubricate her, all over. I will forever be an ass man and hers is to die for.

I take my cock and slowly place my cock at her rim. Going easy. I know it's her first time. I push in as she tightens. I still. "Easy baby, I'll go slow, just relax. Let me make you feel good." I push deeper. I still again and let her relax. Holding back my restraint. I bring my hand down and start to rub her nub. She relaxes. I go slow grinding in her, when I see she can take it, I speed up. God, I've enter Valhalla! I go faster, grinding harder and a steady rate while I viscously rub at her clit. I pull on her nub back and forth while pumping earnestly in her bum. God she feels good. I go faster and I'm loosing control. I lean down down to bite her neck. Bring my lips to her head and say "cum for me baby!" As I'm steadily grinding into her ass. She clenches and screams Yes! Yes! Yes! And cums. I don't stop. I can't. I keep grinding in her hard. I pull her hair back and lose it! Releasing into my Valhalla!!i think I literally have gone there. It's the best sex I've ever had and all before noon! She's my weakness. I lean down to her.

"You ok baby?" She nods breathlessly. I rub her back. "Such a good girl, you did so well." I tell her as climb off the bed and head for the bathroom. I dispose of the condemn and wash myself. Grab a towel and wet it and head back to Kyra. I clean her up. Dispose of the towel and climb in the bed next her. I cover us up and slide her over to me.

"You ok?" I ask her. "More than ok, Damon, I'm great." I push the hair away from her face and kiss her neck. "Did I make you feel better?" I ask I'm a bit nervous and anxious. "Yes, so much better." She rolls over and looks at me. "Don't worry, I'm fine," she slides her finger down my face. I love her touching me. But only only her. She's the only one I will allow to do it. I love her. I'm a love sick fool.

"Kyra?" I'm about to say it. I'm scared that she won't feel the same. I feel like a damn coward. "I love you, Kyra," I sigh "you don't have to say it back, I just wanted you to know, I love you and I will do anything for you, spitfire." She looks at me so tenderly. I see tears in her eyes. "I love you too Damon. So much." I let out the breath I've been holding and I kiss her. She loves me? A monster. How can she love a monster? But I'll take it. I don't deserve it. But I will gladly take it and prove to her everyday that I love her. No one else, but her. Just her.

"Do you want to get up? Or sleep? I'm down for whatever." She giggles and damn those dimples. My love. My heart.

"Sleep of you don't mind. I've had a long night and a very remarkable morning. I'm tired." She rolls over and I bring her close to me. "Sleep, spitfire, I'm not going anywhere." I kiss her neck. She smells so good. Like strawberries. No. I'm not going anywhere. I don't why Tuck did.

Damn Tuck! He left her alone. Hurt her. What's with that asshole? She was in danger and he just left her. Claims that he loves her. I'm having my doubts. Though I see it in his eyes. His reactions. Yea, he may love her, but he's an idiot. Plain and simple.

Kyras soft snores make me laugh. I rub my nose in her hair. I'll protect her. I'll keep her safe. I have too. It's what I have to do. Nothings going to happen to her.

I hear commotion outside the door but I'm not leaving her side. I know the doors locked. They can see her when she's awake. Right now she's mine. Only mine. She needs a break.

The door knob rattles but I pay it no mind. They can damn well wait. I snuggle Kyra closer. Wrapping her right against me. All goes quiet outside the door. I close my eyes and sleep. My last thought is of Kyra and how did I get so lucky.

Or blessed

Jax

—————Julian and I return. Tired from the heat and worried. We go to the kitchen and grab a drink. I finish and throw the drink in the trash missing and go to pick it up. Water spilt on the floor and bust my ass. Julian laughs at me. "Prick you could me!" I tell Julian. He comes over and holds out his hand I take it and we laugh. We hear moaning coming from Kyras room. We both walk to door and listen. Damon is commanding Kyra to finger herself. I try the handle to open the door but it's locked. I look at Julian and he has heat In his eyes. He has the same look I do. He looks me up and down and licks his lips. My dick gets hard instantly. Picturing temptress and Damon and what they're doing. Salivating at Julian.

We hear grunts coming from Tucks room. Probably masturbating about Kyra. Julian looks at me and smiles"Everyone's getting lucky." Yea everyone but us. He looks at me and after a second Julian reaches for the back of my head and kisses me. Hard. Are tongues are clashing and I don't resist. I've never been with a man, but this is not unwelcome. Kyras throws of passion has me already hard and ready to go.

He breaks away from me and looks at me with a question in his eyes "you sure?" Am I? Hell a fuck is a fuck. I grab his hand and take him to my room. I open and shut the door and we are on each other like there's no tomorrow. Kissing and removing our clothes. Tossing them all over the room. I drag him to the bed. I lay on top of him. Kissing him all over.

I catch my breath, pulling a way and look at him "I've never done this before. What do I do?" He smiles. Reaches over to his drawer and pulls out a condemn and a tube of something. "It's lube, it will make it easier, smoother. Relax and let me do the work baby." Baby? No one's ever called me baby. I like it.

He places me on me knees and his head lowers to my cock. He looks at me "close your eyes and enjoy, let me do all the work." I oblige.

He dips his head and his mouth circles my cock. Licking and bobbing. It feels so good. I'm hard as a fucking rock. He circles around the tip, licking the precum. Going down my shaft then releasing it with a pop.

"Turn around and bend over." I hesitate and he notices. "It's ok, I'm about to pop that ass cherry, just relax and breath, baby. Let daddy make you feel good." Hmmm I'm about to bust from his dirty talk. I turn and bend over, ass in the air. He rubs a cold lotion on my ass. Puts on a condemn. "I'll go slow, don't tense, just let me ease in, let me show you what my dick can do." Damn just do it before I explode. He eases into me. He's going slow. It's a bit uncomfortable and tense. "Relax, baby boy. Think of Kyra. Her wet little pussy, shiny and pink. Think of you slipping your huge dick inside her." While he was talking I didn't notice, he was all the way in. Picturing Kyra and her and cunt. Distracting me.

He starts moving, slow at first, i edge him to move faster. I push back on him. He starts pumping faster. Oh the feeling of his dick in me is good. He reaches over and grabs my cock. Pumping me as he's grinding me from behind. Faster and faster. Julian grunts. "You. Like. My. Big. Dick?" "Tell daddy you like it baby boy!" As he grinds. "Yes daddy I like it! I love it! Faster! Faster!" He stops. Wtf!? "Say please," what? Are you kidding me? "Please daddy go faster! Faster! Please!" He starts again grinding. Pumping. Fast and hard. "Scream my name baby boy! Let them hear who fucks you best." Yes! Yes! I'm about to unload. He's pumping and his balls are slapping me and I can't take it anymore. At my release I scream his mother fucking name. "JULIAN! YES!"

We crash down. Panting and satisfying. "Damn Jax, your ass is gold." I laugh at him. Never thought I could be satisfied from a man's touch. A man's dick. "Does this mean I'm gay?" He laughs. "No baby boy, this means your satisfied. So am I." We both laugh. He pulls out slowly and goes to clean up. I can't move. I'm satiated. I feel happy. I have the best of both worlds.

Julian comes to me with a wet cloth and washes my penis. I just watch him. He's taking care of me and it feels right for some reason. "Do you think Kyra would do a threesome?" I ask him. He smiles and has a twinkle in his eye. "Oh I know she will." Uhm and that's something I damn sure wanna try.

He comes to bed and he actually wants to cuddle me. I let him. Can I love a man? Like a boyfriend? If I can then Julian would be the one. I'm not rushing it. I'll just enjoy the moment like I always have. He kisses my forehead. "You ok?" He ask. Am I? I really liked it so yea I guess I am. "More than ok." I look at him and smile and kiss him.

I really hope Kyra is into this, I won't let her go, but now I don't know if can let Julian go either.

————————————————————————   Tim

Night has fallen and I'm elated. It's time. I've been waiting patiently all day. I snap my fingers and I'm back in the witches realm. It's dark and humid outside. There's a light in the window and I peek in. Tuck, Julian and Jax are on the couch talking. Kyra is in the kitchen. Cooking up her men something to eat, how quaint. I don't see Damon but I hear his heartbeat. He's in the house somewhere. Probably still asleep. I laugh with evil intent. I go around to the back so I can sneak up on them quietly. I edge my way into the house. Their so unassuming. It's too easy. I clap my hands loudly. The guys jump up and turn. Kyra drops a knife. Here we go.

"Good evening leaches. I have returned to claim my prize." I look at Kyra "come here slut!" I command. The guys try to come at me. I wave my hand freeze then in their spots. They can't move anything but their eyes and mouth. I want them to enjoy this as much as me. Kyra doesn't move. She's scared. Awe little kitty is scared! Just how I want her. I crook my finger and as I do I bring her to me. Her eyes are wide and going back and forth.

"Leave her the fuck alone!" Screams Tuck. I look at him. "Why do you care? You don't even want her!" I laugh "but I do and your gonna watch and enjoy. Then when I'm done. I'm going to rip her limb from limb, why you hear her cries and knowing there's not a damn thing you can do about it!" I sneer. This is going to be fun.

"You touch her and I'll kill you dammit, I'll break every bone in your damn body!" Jax screams. Tsk tsk"There's nothing you can do but watch little guy. Watch me ravish her. Punish her. Fuck her!!" I roar with laughter. I haven't had this much fun in decades. I'm shaking with anticipation. I walk over to Kyra "Awe my sweets, it's time to play. Do you want to play a game?" I run my finger over her breast. "I want you to run. Run fast. I love the chase and you're my prey. I'm the big bad mother fucking wolf and you my sweets.....are my dinner!"

"RUN! NOW!" I roar. She takes off out the door. I laugh and look at the guys. "I won't keep you waiting long, when I return, your fun will start." I walk over to Tuck. I look him up and down. I reach down unzip his pants and pull out his cock. It's limp in my hands. Disappointing. I look at him. "Don't you wish you fucked her? Now you won't get a chance. Cause that bitch is all mine!" I laugh and take off after my prey. Before I exit I turn to them.

"Don't worry, I'll take really good care of her. I'll have her screaming my name in no time." I sneer and take off.

I exit into the town. Look around. It's totally dark and quiet. I listen for her heart. She's a distance away but I can hear her.

"Here kitty, kitty, I'm coming to get you. Pretty little kitty. Where are you? Come here kitty and let me lick you!" I chase after her. The hunt is so much fun. The fear. The sweat. The climax! I love it all.

"I'm getting closer! Better run pretty kitty. Before the big bad gets you!" I taunt. "I can't wait to taste you pretty kitty. Would you like me to taste you?" She's around the building. I can smell her fear. It smells amazing. I jump around the corner. She backtracks and runs back to the house. Yes! Just where she needs to be. We need to put on a show after all.

I head down the road. "There's nowhere to go kitty, no way out. You are mine and I want my prize." I'm running back to the house. She's there. I hear her. I enter again slowly. The guys are still there frozen. I look for Kyra.

"Pretty kitty, come out to play, it's time to put in a show for your lovers. It's time to die!" I want to see her blood flow from her veins. I want to hear her screams. I want her.

I see her. She's in front of her men. Holding a knife. Trying to put on a brave front. It's sweet. "Awe kitty, you can't hurt me. That little knife won't do a thing to me. But it's a good try. Now drop it and come here and let me show you what a good time really means." It's time to play. I walk over to her. She tries to stab me in my chest. I grab her wrist and turn it. I make her drop the knife. Too easy. She's so tiny. She's no match for me.

I turn her around to face her men. I'm holding both her hands behind her back. I lean down and lick her neck and sniff her hair. I whisper in her ear. "I got you kitty, look at them. They can't help you. You're all mine now. Awe don't cry. It will be fun. At least.....for me." I snicker.

"Don't fucking touch her! Get away from her you ass!" Yells Julian. "That the best you got?" I laugh.

"Let her go, please, we will do anything you ask....just....let her go." Tuck says. He's crying. Why is crying?

"Tears Tuck? You act as if you love her. I know for a fact you don't. So why cry for her? You do as much damage to her as I'm about too. Maybe you'd like to join? Heh? That could be fun." Could be. Maybe "but you see Tuck, I don't share! She's all mine now." Something clicks in his face. A realization perhaps. Too late now.

I grab kitty and slam her down on the couch. I rip off her shirt. I turn to look at them. "Ready guys?" I ask

Cause I am!

Damon

Two persons point of view. Graphic and sexual scenes. 18+ Please enjoy. Vote and comment

I hear him. I'm hiding behind the wall. Biding my time. He won't get her. I won't let him. He keeps talking. Rambling on. Why he hasn't looked for me I don't know. But I do know I'm going to kill him.

Kyra runs past me out the door. I start to go after her, but hesitant. He wants to put on a show. So he will be back. I run to the guys.

"Damon go after him. He's gonna kill her!" Jax says. "Not yet he won't. He wants to put on a show. He won't do it unless we can we watch." I look at back at door. "Go get her Damon, why the fuck are you just standing there?" Tuck screams.

I look at Tuck. "Why is your dick out?" He groans. It would be hilarious, if it weren't for the circumstances.

"Quit playing around. Go save her!" Julian screams.

"Shhh...shut up! Dammit. I'm gonna save her and kill him. Don't worry. I got a plan." I hear running, so I go and hide behind the island. Hoping he doesn't see me.

This dumb ass just keeps rattling on. Why do the bad guys talk so much? I see him throw Kyra on the couch. He rips off her shirt. "Ready guys?" He says. I can't wait any longer. I ease slowly behind the couch. I have my switchblade in my hand. I reach over the couch and slash his throat. Ear to ear. He's gurgling. Blood splatters all over Kyra, me and the couch. Krya kicks him off and stands up.

"He said a knife can't kill him!" Kyra screams. I look to the guys and their moving now. They rush over to Tim. "Damon help!" Jax yells. I rush over and we all grab his head. Kyra throws Tuck a knife. He starts sawing at his neck and we all start pulling and yanking. Blood splatters everywhere. We rip his head off. Breaking his spine.

"Is that enough?" Ask Julian. Hell I don't know. We're all covered in blood and breathing hard. Tim's head lies next to him on the floor. It's a Graphic scene. I look at Kyra and she's on her knees covered in blood and crying.

"Tuck, take care of Kyra. Jax, Julian let's get rid of the body and clean this shit up!" Tuck goes to Kyra and picks her up they head off to her room.

We get to work.

——————————-   Tuck

She's traumatized.

I carry her bridal style into the bathroom. I run on the shower and take off my clothes. I reach over and take her clothes off. She's not speaking. Motionless. Tears are streaming down her face. I get in the shower and drag her with me. I grab a sponge and soap. I place her under the water and start washing her. She just stands there.

I wash her arms and stomach. I then go to her legs. I wash her entire body. The blood cascades down the drain. I place her under the shower and wet her hair I wash and condition it. I rinse it out. The entire time. She doesn't speak. She shows no emotion.

"Come back to me sugar," she finally looks at me. She's still frightened and looks lost. I cut the shower off after washing myself and get out. I grab two towels and wrap one around her and then me. I carry to her bed. She sits on the edge and bows her head. I grab a brush and brush her hair.

I go to look for her some clothes. I find a nightgown and panties. I bring them to her and put them on her. She doesn't speak. I lay her down and cover her up. I just stare at her.

I run to my room and grab some boxers and put them on. I head back to her room on my way I see the guys have disposed of Tim's body and head but there's still blood on the floor. I shake my head.

I enter her room and she's laying in the same position. I don't hesitate, I go to lay beside her and cover up. "Sugar, are you ok? Talk to me baby!" I plead with her.

She rolls over and looks me she breaks down sobbing. I grab her and wrap my arms around. I hold on to her for dear life. Letting her get it all out. She falls asleep crying. I grab her tighter and drift off to sleep.

—————————

I wake up to hear her closing the bathroom door. It's still dark out. She crawls back into bed and covers up. I grab her and pull her to me. "You ok?" I ask. She nods her head. "Talk to me sugar please." I caress her back with one hand and move her hair with my other. She sighs.

"I'm fine Tuck, go to sleep." She looks up at me I see her pain and sadness. She's so beautiful and I just can't hold back any more. I need her.

I roll her over and start kissing her. Our mouths collide in heated passion. Tongues thrashing and I'm groping. I take her gown off and throw it on the floor. I kiss her down her neck and suck her skin in. Marking her. She's mine! I ease down and take her breast in my mouth. Sucking and licking. I bite down her nipple and release it to go to the next one. I lower my hand and lower it down her panties. I place my finger on her clit rotating it. I suck and bite on her nipple.

I lower my self and take off her panties. I remove my boxers. She stares at my cock and her eyes go wide. I laugh. Yea baby it's all yours. "May I" I ask her for her permission. She nods her head and that's all I need. I crash down on her pussy. I lick and suck and lick more. I suck in her clit. I put to fingers in her opening and bend them. She's moaning and gyrating uncontrollably.

I put my hand on her stomach to hold her still. I dive back in. I kiss her thighs and suck the skin in. I go to the next thigh and do the same. I return to her mound and lick from her bottom to the top. I'm about to shoot my wad. She taste like honey dew and sex. "I burn for you, Kyra."

I raise up and start kissing her again letting her taste her own sweetness. I grab her hand and put it on my cock. "This is what you do to me. I have been hard for weeks. This is all for you. Can I fuck you?" She whispers yes and I'm a goner.

I place my cock at her entrance and slowly slide in. I want to enjoy every inch. I entered Eden. God she's delectable. I start to moving my hips. Going faster I set up and grab her legs. I place one on my shoulder and the other around my hips. It's go time. I start pushing deeper. Harder. Faster. I'm pushing at a record high. I'm going so fast and I can't get enough. Her breast are bouncing back and forth and I grab one kneading it. I punch her nipple.

"I. Fucking. Love. You." I grind out as I push harder into her core. She moans and she's pulsating on my cock. Clinching like a vise. I lose it. "FUCK!" I scream as squirt my seed into her. She cries out my name. The best sound in the world.

I fall on top her. Climaxing as I go. I pant and try to catch my breath. I stay inside her. I look up into her eyes. She's smiling and radiant. Damn this woman is my queen.

She wiggles and I get hard again. Her eyes widen and I laugh. I grab her hands and place them above her head. I kiss her. "I love you Kyra. I've loved you for awhile. I was a damn fool not to admit it. I'm sorry I hurt you. I will never do it again. I need you in my life. Please forgive me and stay with me. I'm not talking about just now. I'm talking about forever." I look at her and she's crying. Damn I hurt again. Then she surprises me. She rolls herself on top of me. Leans down and whispers in my ear.

"Damn Tuck i love you too baby. I have for awhile. I do forgive you. Just please don't hurt me again. I don't think I can take it." I'm one happy mother fucker. I raise up and kiss her and she starts gyrating on top of me. She grabs her breast and pinches her nipples. She brings her finger up to her mouth and licks it. She takes her finger down to her clit and starts playing with it. Fuck! I start pumping into her again. She's bouncing on my dick like a pogo stick. I grab her ass and raise her up and down. Pumping into her with all my might. I reach over and rub her clit. I pinch it and pull. She cums all over fingers and cock.

We crash together in a heap of sweat and hormones. She rolls over releasing my seed all over me and her. Then it hits me. Fuck. No condemn. I was to lost in the moment. I didn't think. Fuck!I turn to Kyra "Sugar, we forgot the condemn." She freaks. Jumps off the bed. Naked and pacing back forth. Damn if I'm not hard again.

"It's ok, calm down. Sugar." Trying to relax her. I get off the bed and walk to her. I don't think she heard me. I grab her shoulders and turn her toward me.

"Kyra! Calm down it's ok. Everything's going to be fine. Just relax. Breath baby." She looks at me and blows a gasket.

"CALM DOWN! I CANT CALM DOWN! WHAT THE HELL TUCK!"She's beautiful when she's mad. I laugh. I can't help it.

"Why are laughing? This is serious Tuck! What if I get pregnant? What if I catch a disease?" I bristle at the last comment. She catches what she said and turns to me. Wraps her arms around my waist. "I'm sorry. I'm sorry. I didn't mean it. I know you wouldn't hurt me. I'm so sorry." She sounds like a kid. I laugh again.

"Kyra I don't have a disease and if you get pregnant then, it's ok. I'll be there for you and the baby. I always will." I lift her chin up to look at me. I kiss her forehead. "I wouldn't mind being a dad sugar." She seems surprised. She shakes her head.

"No Tuck, I won't trap you like that. I'll take care of it. You don't need to worry." She turns and goes to the bathroom. Wtf? She is not talking about getting rid of my child is she? Fuck no! I go to the bathroom and slam open the door. She yelps and turns to me.

"You are not getting an abortion if you're pregnant. That is my child and I have a say so in it!" She laughs. She actually laughs.

"I would never do that! I was talking of taking care of the child myself Tuck. I could never, ever do that." I feel dumb. I laugh. I walk up to her.

"You do realize that we're arguing over a pregnancy that's not even confirmed yet. Right?" We both laugh. We clean up. She puts her gown and panties back on. I put on my boxers. We climb into bed and cover up. She lays on my chest while embrace her.

I love this woman. I love her with my entire heart and soul. Pregnant or not I want to be with her. I'm don't running away anymore. I'll share as long as I get to love her too.

"Marry me Sugar."

————————

Kyra

Marry me sugar.

Oh holy hell, I think my uterus just exploded.

What do I say to that? I love him, I know I do. But marry him? Is he asking me because I could be pregnant? Because he loves me? He's been so up and down lately. I feel like I'm in an elevator with him. Never reaching a destination. I look up at him and sigh out deeply.

"No, Tuck, I can't marry you. Please don't be upset. I love you, I do. So much. But I also love the others as well. You know this. One night of sex. Hot and very good sex, I might add," I giggle. "Doesn't mean you should marry me and if I am pregnant. Well we can go from there. Ok?" I hate doing this to him. I know he may reject me yet again. I fear it.

He gets up and goes for the door as he reaches for the doorknob he turns to me "Kyra, I asked you because I love you. Not because of sex or that you might be pregnant. Because I want you to be wife. To love, honor, and cherish you, always." And with that declaration he leaves the room.

I'm tormented and confused. It's been six weeks and these guys have turned my world upside down. We've been lost. Confused. Isolated. Hurt. Almost killed and we have loved. It seems like too much. I start to cry, yet again. I feel like that's all I ever do anymore is cry. How am I, one girl, one woman, suppose to handle all four of them?

I lie back down and fall into a fitful sleep.

— — — — — — — — —

Im running through a Forrest. It's cold and dark. I hear owls and the leaves crunch under my feet. Im alone. I keep running from what I don't know. I just know I need to run.

I see a light in between two trees. Casting its glow amongst them. I run to it. It's a cabin looming by lake. It's old and the shutters are falling. I get closer, look in the window. I see a Tuck and woman arguing. She throwing her hands around and her face is red. Tuck is upset and keeps trying walk off but she won't let him.

Their voices grow louder. "Bring him back!" Tuck yells and the woman begins to cry. I step closer. "No, I will not! Not until you marry me!" He gets more agitated. "I will never marry you, you're a vile woman, now bring him back to me!" She shakes her head. I step closer almost touching the glass. A twig breaks. I look inside and she turns head and walks to the window. I take off running. The last thing I heard was Tuck screaming Casandra!

————————————

I wake up sweating and panting. I can't breath. I stumble out of bed and open the door with a slam. Julian sees me and rushes over. "Breath, cookie, in and out. Relax. Deep breaths," I calm myself, my breathing slows. "Better?" I nod my head. "I need Tuck! Where's Tuck?" I yell out. Jumping up and running to the kitchen. Julian on my heels. I get there and see Jax on the couch in the living area. Damon's eating breakfast and Tuck is missing.

"Where's Tuck?" I'm frantic. They all look at me worried. "He's out by the pool." Damon said. I take off to the pool, they all follow. I see Tuck on a lounge chair. His elbows are on his knees and his hands is on face. "TUCK!" I run to him. He looks up surprised. Worry on his face. I grab his hands. I start rambling.

"She did it! At first I thought it was you. Then I remembered your brother was your twin. They were fighting and yelling and she did it Tuck! She did this to us!" I'm frantic. I'm looking at everyone.

"Slow down sugar," he grabs my face. "Who did what? Go Slower, explain." So I do. I tell them all about my dream. In vivid detail. I see doubt on their faces. I'm not getting through to them. How can I make them believe me?

"It's true, it's all true. She did it. Somehow, someway, she put us all here. She destroyed our lives. All so she can marry Chuck! Please believe me." I'm pleading. They still look doubtful. How can they doubt me?

"You mean to tell me, that you all believe Tim was a demonic being and that we," i point to all of us "are trapped in a desolate wasteland. But you don't believe my dream?" I yell. Screw this. I jump up go to my room. Slam the door and lock it! I grab some clothes. Head to the shower and wash up. I put on my white tank top. Blue Jean shorts and shoes. I grab a bag and pack my clothes. I'm moving to the second floor. I'm done. They don't believe me. They think I'm lying. I'll figure this out on my own. I don't need them. I grab my toiletries and head back out.

There all in the living room now. I ignore them. Turn down the hall and climb the stairs. I find a decent room. Third door down. I unpack my things and sit on the bed.

Defeated. Somehow, I will figure this out. I will get us back home if it's the last thing I do!

————————————Days crept by slowly. I remained in my room. I discovered a bookshelf full of books and have been spending my time away from the guys, reading. I don't mind being alone, I'm use to it. They've tried to engage me in small talk. Asking if I'm ok? I just nod, grab my food and return to my room, reading. It's an escape from the pain they caused me. Not believing me. Thinking I'm crazy.

I've never lied to them. I never once doubted them. But they doubt me. I feel heartbroken and isolated. Though I may be use to it, it still saddens me to no end.

Tuck refuses to talk to me. Just gives forlorn looks and turns away.

Jax tries his hardest. He and Julian have formed an relationship with each other. I'm happy for them, but I miss them.

Damon is secluded. I rarely see him. He hides away like me. What he's doing I have no idea, but they all seem content with me keeping my distance these days.

I close my book with a sigh. I love Dean Koontz, but he can't hold my attention today.

There's a knock at my door. The first one in days. It startled me and I dropped my book with a yelp. They don't wait for me to answer. Jax and Julian standing in the doorway, staring and not saying a word.

"What?" I ask them as I retrieve my book from the floor. They don't answer. They walk on in. Jax turns and locks the door. I squint my eyes at them. I'm not in the mood for their games.

"Get out!" I tell them. But neither is budging. Their just standing there arms crossed and looking at me. I get a bit nervous. "Get out! Now!" Still they don't budge.

Jax comes over to me grabs my book. Tosses onto the dresser and turns to me.

"We're done with the silent treatment temptress. We want to talk." I huff out. Now they want to talk?

"There's nothing to say, you don't believe me, that's fine, I'm fine, just leave!" I bounce on bed. Crossing my legs and arms. Raising my chin at the two.

They sigh and look at me, defeated. I won't give them an inch. Not until they apologized. I'm tired of being the little mouse that scurries away. That's not me, not anymore.

I stand go to the door, unlock and open it, "GO!" Julian shakes his head. Walks to the door. Shuts and locks it again.

"No, cookie, we're gonna talk and you are gonna listen." Fine, I go back to bed, sit on the edge, adjust my minidress and look at them waiting. "So, talk, then leave." I feel like I'm sufficiently stating want I want. Let them explain and leave, then I'll go back to Mr. Koontz, in my little cell of a room.

Julian comes and sits beside me. He grabs my hand, but I jerk it away. I'm still angry and don't want to give in. Jax comes to stand before me. He kneels down in front me. He place a hand on my knee to brace himself. I move my knee away. He sighs, pinches his nose and shakes his head.

"We're sorry cookie. We're sorry we didn't believe you. We're sorry that we hurt you." He goes to slide a strand of my hair out of my face. I swat his away. Saying you're sorry is one thing. Truly being sorry is another.

"Ok, you said it, no you can leave." I go stand but Jax pushes me back in place. "We need to talk, no more hiding. No more running. We are gonna fix this.....we miss you Kyra." I miss them too. I look down at my hands and twiddle my fingers. "Why" I whisper to them.

"Why what?" Jax ask. "Why didn't you believe me?" I look up at Jax. I'm heartbroken but I will not cry. Not again.

"I don't know, it just seemed so far fetched. Dreams aren't reality temptress. But we talked and after all that we've been through, it doesn't sound so far fetched as we thought at first. Please forgive us. Come out of your room and we will all make it up to you. Please."

My wall is crumbling. I will not cry. I'm not the mouse anymore but I do miss them. I'm so alone without them. I look at Julian and he half smiles. He's rubbing my back in semi circles. He reaches his hand out to my hand and I finally let him touch me.

I look back to Jax and he places his hand back on my knee. I don't move this time. "I missed you guys so much. I've been so lonely. I miss your smiles and laughter. I just wish you would have trusted me more." Believe me!

"I am so damn sorry cookie, I will never doubt you again. We will never doubt you again. Can you please forgive us. We need you back." He looks so pure and sweet. My wall start to crack and it tumbles down.

"Yes, I forgive you. Just never ever doubt me again. It hurts too much." They both smile. Relief showing on their faces. Jax leans forward to kiss me. But I turn my head. He looks shocked, but I need to ask.

"Uhm...aren't you guys like dating now?" I don't want to come in between them. They look so cute together. I don't want to get in their way. Jax laughs and sits back on the floor.

"Yes, yes we are. But we both want to be with you also. We love you and I for one will not be giving you up." Jax states with determination. I turn to Julian searching his eyes for an answer. He smiles, and squeezes my hand.

"We both love you and want you in our lives. You already live in our hearts. Does it bother you?" He points at Jax "that Jax and I are together? Is that something you would be interested in?" I've never thought about it before. But I love them and if we can be together, couple or threesome, I wouldn't care, just as long as we love each other and share that love.

"No, it doesn't. I love you both also, if you'll have me, that is. It doesn't bother me if it doesn't bother you."They smile from ear to ear. I wonder how this will work?

"How will this work?" I point at all us "between us, I mean?" They look at each other, then back to me.

Let us show you.

——————————Please vote and comment Thanks for reading pretties.

JULIAN

————

Game on! "Take off your clothes," I say to both of them. We all start stripping. Standing nude, I turn to Kyra, "get on the bed." She jumps on the bed, trying to contain her excitement. "Climb on top of her." I say to Jax. He more than complies. It's been way too long. We're both extremely excited.

He looks at me for direction with his eyes full of wonderment. "Chow down, baby boy!" He doesn't wait a second. Jax is eating her like it's his last meal. I go to Kyra and fondle her breast. I lean down to kiss her. I get lost in her kiss. Moaning and full of anticipation. I lower my head to her breast and suck on it hard. Licking and nibbling. I take my hand and dive down to her clit. While Jax is fingering her wet pussy.

I raise up and go to get two condoms. I hand one to Jax and one for myself. We put them on. I get on the bed and lower myself behind Jax. I put my hand on Kyras pussy and lap up her juices. I take it and rub it on Jax's ass. Preparing him. "Put your cock inside of her, baby boy." He grabs his cock and enters Kyra fully. "Stop," I place my cock at Jax's asshole and enter. God he's still tight. "I'm going to make Baby boy here, fuck you at my pace Kyra. He isn't in control, I am. If you want us to stop, use a safe word. What's your safe word baby?" I ask her huskily.

"Eternal" it's fitting. Like the Eternal Flames song she sang to us.

"Here we go cookie, ready for a ride?" She nods. I start grinding into Jax's ass. Pushing him into Kyras pussy. I'm in control. He can only fuck her as fast as I want him to. I feel like a fucking God.

I'm pumping into him hard. Making him push into Kyra at a brisk fast pace. Their both groaning, lost up in their desirable haze. "Rub her clit baby boy," he reaches to rub her nub. Forcefully rubbing and pulling on it. I reach down and massage his balls all the while I'm pumping forcefully into my man's ass. Having control over how he fucks her is exhilarating. I go faster. Hitting him with all of my force. Kyra is losing her shit. Jax is on edge and I'm about to blow my load.

Grinding and pumping. Faster and faster. "Oh yes, yes, that's it. Right there! YES!" Screams Kyra as she comes to her heated climax. I'm still pumping into Jaxs ass not letting up. I gyrate my hips and hit that sweet spot. Jax yells and I follow right behind him, "Fuck yes!" I roar out when my cum explodes all within him.

We're now in a dog pile. Breathing rapidly and panting hard. I remove my self from Jax and dispose of my used condom. Jax then does the same. "Wow, that was just, wow" Kyra laughs. Her breast bouncing with her giggles and my dick goes hard again. She's a damn wanton. I can't get enough of her. I jump on top of her and start kissing down the crook of her neck hungrily.

I reach my hand down to her succulent breast and start kneading them. She's moaning and moving her hips against my hardened dick. I can't resist. I enter her and start grinding into her maddeningly. I keep pumping into her sweet cunt ferociously. My appetite for her seems to have no control. I roll her over so that now she's on top of me. Jax suddenly climbs behind her and starts rubbing her sensitive clit. Pushing her top down on my chest. He places his cock at her rear and damn! He enters her. I can feel his dick through her thin barrier rub my mine. I let out a needy groan as I start thrusting up into her cunt again along with Jax pivoting into her ass simultaneously. He's in and I'm out. Grinding and pounding into her. She's taking it like a damn pro. Best fucking sex ever! "You like both of us in you, cookie?

I can feel Jax's cock rub against mine. Do we fill you up? Do we make you complete?" She moans. Jax is not letting up. I grab her hips and start bouncing her on my throbbing dick.

She is my addiction, my drug. "Fuck, temptress, your ass is on fire!" Jax roars. He reaches down and grabs ahold my balls tenderly while he's squeezing them softly I lose it all over again. Squirting my seed into her, my balls are about to explode. Jax keeps going. He grabs her shoulder and pulls her up then bites down on her neck. He then reads his back and screams "FUCK!" And fills her up completely. Kyra suddenly goes limp on top of me as Jax then crashes lightly onto her back.

"That was fucking awesome!" States Jax and I have to agree with him on that. He abruptly pulls out then heads off into the bathroom. Kyra raises herself off of me and rolls over on the mattress. Jax suddenly reappears with a wet cloth in his hand. After we get all cleaned up I roll over and pull her closer to me. Jax gets in on other side of the bed while wrapping his arms around her mod section.

This is my heaven. My world. Right here on this bed. I couldn't be happier. I love them both. More than I would have ever imagined.

"You ok, cookie?" She stretches "yes I am." She laughs. "But we forgot the condoms." I still. Oh shit! We're fucked! I look at Jax and the fucker is smiling devilishly over at me. Devious prick! No doubt thinking she's ours now no matter what. He's always loved her. Always wanted her. Even though I was the first. He claimed her from the beginning. Nothing was gonna stop that asshole from getting what he wanted and that was definitely her.

"It's all good temptress, we just lost control." We huh? Im the one who jumped her. Im the one who didn't think and I'm the one who would father this child. I feel like a jackass. Well it can't be helped mow. I love her and want to be with her always. A child makes no difference to me. Being a dad doesn't sound too bad at all to me.

"It's ok, Tuck did the same thing." She yawns. What? Jax looks at me all confused. Tuck never said anything. Now it could be me or him that could be the dad to this supposed child?

"Did Damon use a condom?" I need to know. She doesn't answer. He soft snores shows that she's asleep. I look at Jax. He's staring at me. Curiosity all over his face.

"That's fucked up, I thought we'd at least talk about who wants to be dad first." He's not to happy about this. Maybe he wanted to be first. But he's the youngest out of allus. He still has time.

"Doesn't matter to me as long as we're happy. We will all be the child's father. Not just one. We're a family unit. We will thrive as one." That's the way I see it anyway. Hope the others do as well.

"Yes but if it's Tucks you really think he would share his child? He didn't even want to share her! There's gonna be a major conflict here. He's too possessive to share anything. Hell I'm surprised they slept together." I'm not. I've seen the way he looks at her. The way he longs for her. He can't hide that shit from me.

"Well I'm not leaving her even if it is his! He's just going to have to get use to it or piss off. She's ours and I won't back down." The prick can just get over hisself. I'm not going anywhere.

"Me either Julian, but it will end up being a fight and we will also have us to think about. Our relationship. I'm not trying to be a dick, but you know how he is?" I do but he doesn't know how I am.

"I don't care. I'm not giving up on her and that's that Jax!" I can't imagine losing her. This is ridiculous! She moves and groans then rolls over. I lower my voice "she's my cookie Jax, Tuck will not keep me away, us away. I won't let him!" I can't.

"I'm on your side Julian, I feel the same damn way! I love her too, but we have to be practical. If it's his child we have no say!" He whispers aggressively. I feel like I'm being ripped apart. In a matter of moments I go from bliss to heartbreak. I grab Kyra tighter. Would I have to let her go? Would Tuck do this to us?

"It's a moot point. We don't know if she's pregnant or not and we don't know how Tuck feels. All I know is we have to think about this logically," then adds "I wish it was me." I can't deal.

"Well it could be mine, if she does get pregnant. So there's that hope. Until we know, let's just pray it is mine and not his. That's the better outcome. For us anyway." He nods his head.

"Either way, we should talk to Tuck. Find out where he stands about all this. He may not even want a child. Who knows ? He may fool us and actually join our unit. Miracles can happen." I doubt that but we will see. No matter what though I'm not losing her. I can't I just can't.

I fall asleep thinking about eternal.

—————————

She's sits on couch with her guitar. Strumming the strings singing like an angel. We all stop in our tracks. Not moving a muscle. Barely breathing.

Her voice lights up my very soul. The melody caressing my heart. The words burn into me. She has a fluorescent glow around her, She's magical. Completely ethereal.

The song Eternal Flames echoes throughout the house. Falling beautifully from her mouth. Every word sends shivers through my entire body.

I'm in love.

I stare at her as she finishes her song. We clap and she turns, shocked we're there. Her captive audience.

Then she disappears. The guitar drops to the floor. The loud crashing sound matches my crashing heart.

She's gone, never to see her again. Her beauty, her smile, her heart.

Kyras gone!

————————

I wake up breathing heavy. Trying to gasp for air. I look over to my side and see Jax asleep snoring. Kyras unfortunately missing.

I jump out of bed racing around the house looking for her.

I stop....I hear music. It's coming from the patio. I run to the door. There she is with the moonlight shining her casting a effervescent glow around her. She's the image of pure light. She's strumming her guitar and humming along. It's a different song this time. One I know but I can't seem to place.

"What's the song you're playing?" She jumps at my voice. Turns to me and smiles. Those damn dimples. I can't get enough. I feel the urge to tell her how deeply she effects me.

"It's Open Arms by Journey it's one of my favorites. You never heard of it? It's a classic." She giggles and goes back to playing.

"Sing it for me, it sounds familiar." She begins to sing.

Lying beside you, here in the dark. Feeling your heartbeat with mine.

And I'm lost. Listening to her golden voice and it's mesmerizing me. I just fell more in the love with this woman. Everything about her swallows me up.

So now I come to you with open arms. Nothing to hide, believe what I say.

I remember the song. She makes it awe inspiring. Every word. every melody feels like home.

She finishes the song and turns to me smiling. We jump when we hear clapping. Tuck comes out of the dark house. A smile on his face. Standing in sweats and nothing else.

"That's my favorite song. I love Steve Perry. You did a wonderful job. Might even be better than his version." Might? It so surpasses it. Way to ruin a moment Tuck! I don't know why I'm angry at him. Well yea, I guess I do. He's a threat to me now. To me and all that I hold dear. I won't let him win. I just simply can't.

I get up tell Kyra goodnight and that we're waiting in bed. Just to put a little rubbing on Tuck. I get up and hit his shoulder as I walk by. He turns to me but I just keep going. To upset to even care. I crash in Kyras bed with Jax still snoring. Feeling angry and somewhat lost.

Even if it is his child. I won't lose her.

I just can't!

————————Thanks for reading prettiesVote and comment

TUCK

Lying beside you here in the dark. Feeling your heart beat with mine.

I will forever remember this moment.

I woke to get a drink, it was hot and the humidity was a bitch. When I went into the kitchen. I heard music. I followed the melody like a drug to my soul. Julian was sitting in a seat beside her. She was playing the guitar and singing my favorite song. It's like she knew. It's like she sung it just for me.

Julian was hypnotized, his eyes never straying from her. I was enraptured by her soulful melody and desirable sounds.

Every note she hit, every line she sung, hit directly to my heart.

So now I come to you with open arms. Nothing to hide, believe what I say.

She was mesmerizing me with her tune.

I fell deeper in love.

When she finished I clapped. This was the moment of my undoing. My very being. I will worship my queen.

I told how great of a job she did and that it was my favorite song. Julian gets up and said a few words to her. That he will be waiting in the room. He walks pass me and bumps my shoulder. I turn to look at him as he walks off.

"What's his problem?" I ask Kyra. She just shrugs her shoulder and puts the guitar down. Propping it on the wall. She turns to me and smiles. I haven't seen that smile in so long. I haven't seen much of her lately, I miss her.

"We need to talk sugar," I tell her as I sit in the chair Julian vacated. I look over at her and I take her hand. I need to touch her. To feel her close. "I'm sorry I didn't believe you, but you must admit Kyra, it does sound a little out there," she's starting to get upset. She scowls and bites her lip. "I'm just saying sugar that it's not that believable, not that I think you're lying, but it's not possible that Casandra can do this. All of this, to us."

I need her to understand that Casandra isn't a nice a person but to do something like this, I just can't picture it. She's not a witch first of all. Plus she's not that vindictive or even that smart.

Instead of letting me explain all this and my way of thinking. She jumps up and literally screams. Loudly. She storms off inside. I realize then that I just made things tremendously worse.

I get up to go search for her. I see her going up the stairs to her room. She slams the door. Hard. I go the door and open it. Julian and Jax are lying on the bed. Both have been woken up by Kyra slamming the door. Wtf? Both of them? I see red!

"What the fuck Kyra? You slept with both of them, at the same time?" Oh boy, did I fuck up. She races over to me and slaps me across the face. Very hard. My face is stinging and I get pissed.

I may have deserved that.

She's packing her clothes and other items. Storming across the room. Julian and Jax are out of bed trying to get her stop, asking what happened. Damon comes to the door. Confused and looking around.

"What the fuck is going on?" Damon ask as he watches Kyra pack her things. She grabs a book tosses it in bag. Ignoring all of us. She bypasses me and Damon and heads down the stairs. We all follow.

She takes off running out the door. We're screaming for her to stop she doesn't listen she keeps going.

"What the fuck did you do"" Julian screams and pushes me. "Back off Julian it's none of your damn business!" I push him back.

"It is my damn business, she's my damn business!" As he points out the door. "This is the last fucking time you get to hurt her. You hear me? The last fucking time!" He punches me in the jaw. He doesn't stop. Three to four punches in Damon and Jax pulls him off me. I stand up and spit out blood onto the floor and wipe my mouth. I stagger a bit.

"You're a prick Tuck! You never stop and think about her feelings! You treat her like shit! Then you fuck her with no damn condom! You don't even care! Stay the fuck away from her! Do hear me! Stay. The. Fuck. Away!" He storms out the door. We're all stunned. His comments hit hard.

"You didn't use a condom? What the fuck is wrong with you? You want to knock her up? Don't you care about what we think? How we feel?" Damon screams at me. No I didn't care and I didn't think.

"I fucked up alright! Is that what you want to hear? I got caught up in it all, I didn't think! Dammit!" I scream. Angrily punching the air. Pacing back and forth.

"Julians right. Just stay away from her you've done enough damage." Jax tells me. I know I have. I feel guilty and angry. I don't need them to tell me how bad I messed up.

"I love her." I tell them. Hoping they will understand, just a little bit. "No you don't. If you did, you wouldn't treat her this way. You would accept her. Believe her. Trust in her. You don't love her. You just wanted her!" States Jax but it's not true. I do love her. I just fuck everything up. All the time.

Jax leaves out the door. In search for her and Julian. I turn to look at Damon. "You understand right? I do love her. It's just so damn hard." I plead for understanding. He looks at the door then to me. "Nope" he pops the p "what I understand is that you need to figure out your shit and stay away from her until you do." He heads out the door also.

I can't stay away from her that's the problem.

I head out the door looking for Kyra. My jaw is aching and throbbing. This is bullshit. I just can't believe that Casandra is responsible for all this. Just so she can have my brother. There are other ways to go about it. She's not a damn witch. A bitch maybe, but not a witch. I need Kyra to understand that. How can I prove to her that it just can't be. There's no way in this world she can could this. That she would do this to me. There just isn't.

I see the guys in front of the old building where the bar use to be. Oh no! She didn't! I run up to them.

"I can't get in, I saw her run in when it was the bar then it changed to this old building again. How did she get in the last time? Do y'all remember?" Pleads Julian. He's frantic. Dude needs to calm down. We did it once before we can do it again.

"She threw something at it.....a water bottle. She threw a water bottle." Jax says. "Go get one" Damon tells him. Jax takes off back to the house.

"What are you doing here? Just leave! We don't need you!" Julian tells me. But I need her. I was just about to say that, but thought better of it. I don't say a word, just turn around and ignore him. He huffs out. Damon puts his hand on my shoulder and I turn to him. He half smiles. Then Jax returns with a the water.

"She threw at the door last time. The top was off and water sprayed all over it. I remember that much." Jax tells us. So he takes off the top and throws it at the building.

Nothing happens.

Not even a glitch. We all stare dumbfounded. Well what now?

Julian goes and bangs on the door. Jax is trying the handle. They can't get it open. Damon takes off back to the house.

Julian screams and turns to me. I'm gearing up for his onslaught. My jaw already hurts. I'm not letting him get another hit. We all turn as we hear Damon returning. He has a crowbar with him. He goes to the door and works to try to get it open. It's not budging. Nothing seems to be working. I'm exasperated. I set on the dirt road. Bringing my knees up to me. After awhile,

Jax and Julian come and sit beside me. Damon still tries to open the door.

"Stop it man, it's not going to work." Jax tells him. Damon throws the crowbar and screams. He walks over to us and plops down beside Jax.

"What are we gong do?" Julian ask. I don't know. No one does. I did this. Yet again and yet again I'm filled with guilt and remorse. Maybe I do need to grow the fuck up.

"What happened Tuck? I left you alone with Kyra on the patio. She was happy. What the hell happened?" I hate this. Now I have I explain how stupid I was. Again. So I tell them. I tell them what I thought about Casandra. About her not being able to be a witch. How she would never do this to me. To us. I tell them everything. How I proposed to Kyra, how she turned me down. How she ripped out my heart. I spill my guts. I poor out my soul.

"Shit! How you can you even believe Casandra after all she has done to you? Manipulated you. How can you not believe Kyra over her? You are one dumb son of bitch!" Damon tells me.

"She thinks you proposed cause she could be pregnant. She told you no, because of that reason alone. Not because she doesn't love you. You idiot!" States Jax he's mad and I don't blame him. But I still can't wrap my head around any of it.

"You know Tuck, if you just took one damn second to listen to her. To really listen to her. We wouldn't be in this mess. You've hurt her over your stupid possessiveness. You hurt her over your dumb ass and very wrong and misguided views of Casandra. You've hurt her over and over again. You, Tuck, do not deserve her. So when we get her back. When we find her. You need to stay the hell away from her. If she is pregnant we will take care of the baby. We will be the child's dad. Not you! Us!" Julian screams at me. Wtf? Hell no!

"That would be child! Not yours! Mine! So back the fuck off and don't tell me what to do!" I tell him

"Oh no Tuck, it could be my child. Not yours! Mine!" He yells and storms off. I stand there shocked. His child? How the?

"What's he talking about? His child?" I ask Jax. He looks down then stands up. Let's out a sigh.

"He forgot to use a condom tonight. Heat of the moment and all that. So yea, it could be his child. That is, if she's pregnant. Well no, I take that back. It could be our child." He points at Damon then at Julian's retreating form. Then he laughs and walks off. They don't go far. I can still see them. Their not leaving the building till she comes out.

I look at Damon. "Y'all's child?" He smiles and gets up. Looks at me dead in the eyes.

"Yep! We're all in. Even if he is the biological pops. We all be the kids fathers. As in, all of us. You need to get that through your thick skull man. She's all of ours. Not just yours. So if that is your child. If she is pregnant? It will still be all of ours, just not yours. Regardless, if your in the picture or not." He said and turns away.

I release a breath. I turn at look at the building and for the first time in a long time, I break down crying like a child. Like a damn kid.

I fucking cried!

——————Thank you pretties. Please vote and comment I would like to mention a new character in this next chapter. His name is Otter and he solves a lot of problems. I just love him.

otter

Multiple povs. Enjoy pretties.

Oh, yes sir. Right away sir, I'll will go there immediately.

I hustle out of the councils office, to grab some supplies for my journey. My clipboard, a pencil or two, my glasses. Wait, where are my glasses. I know I had them this morning. Oh boy, if I'm late, the council will have my head. Oh! Wait there they are. Right on my face. I'm a nervous wreck. It's my first assignment. I'm to go to the witches realm and secure a journey home for five individuals.

Ok I think I have everything. I zap myself there. This place is awful. Dry, dusty, and hot. My allergies can't handle this dust! I cough and wheeze. Jeez. This is awful. I look up and see four giant men staring at me. Oh boy! Here we go.

"Excuse me gentlemen, by any chance are you?....." I pat myself down. Searching for drat pencil. I just had it. Coughing and searching. Oh yes! Behind my ear of course. Drat! "Ok let's see...Tuck, Damon, Julian.... I pronounce it hulian, and Jax?" I look up to see them wide eyed and curious. "Oh I'm sorry, let me introduce myself, I'm Otter, I'm from the supernatural council, I'm councilman's Terregas sectarian. I've come to take you home. Isn't that nice?" I cough again. Drat this awful dust.

"There is also a Kyra, is there not? Where may I find her?" I ask them. She's on the list. She should be here. I raise my eyes to the gentleman and they all sigh. Curious. I cough again. Drat!

"She went into this building and we can't get in. She's trapped in there." Oh my, well no fretting over it. I walk to the building and wave my hand. The building changes to a bar, I presume, looks like one. I turn to the gentleman "shall we?" They looked surprised but enter nonetheless.

"Kyra! Kyra! Cookie, you in here?" Screams one of the gentleman. "Uhm who's cookie? I only have one female on my list and that's a Kyra?" He laughs. "Kyra is cookie" he states. Oh ok. Well drat, then where is she?

A door creaks open and we turn to look. There stands a beautiful woman. Though her hair is mess and her eyes are red. I turn to look at the gentlemen. Relieve is shown on their faces. "Ok well then shall we get started?" They all turn to me. Kyra looks at me confused.

"As I was saying I'm here to return you back home. All of you. You're not suppose to be here. You were banished here by a witch, her name was....." I flip through the pages on my clipboard. What was here name? Oh yes! "By a witch named Casandra Bell." They all gasp. I look up to see all of them looking at at the tallest gentleman with furious faces. "Well as per usual I will do a mind sweep, that is done to erase all of your memories of being here, so there will be no trauma of the situation and of course, so you have no knowledge of the supernatural." They look all mad. Interesting.

"Please don't. Don't take away our memories. We won't say a word. None of us will. I promise." Said the beautiful one. Oh drat, I don't know if I can do that? They have been through so much. I feel guilty. But it's my first assignment. What to do?

"We won't speak of word of this. To anyone. We just....want to remember. To remember each other. You understand right?" She tells me. Well I guess it won't hurt. "You must not tell anyone. If you do we will place you back in the witches realm with no return policy. Understand?" Hoping they won't say anything. I don't usually breaks the rules. But they I have been tormented. We owe them at least that much, I suppose. "We won't! Promise!" She says. I look to the others and they all nod their heads. Ok then. That's settled now let's get them home. I start to send them back but the tall gentlemen interrupts me first.

"Kyra, can we talk?" He looks so forlorn. "No," she looks at me "can we just go? Please?" She looks so sad. I don't know what happened between them; but it is my job to get them home so....

"Ok you will feel a bit dizzy when you reach your destinations; it's common so don't worry. So with that said. It was very nice to meet all of you and we are sorry for the circumstances and awkwardness you had endured. Oh yes one more thing. The witch has been dealt with. She is banished to a prison realm so you won't have to deal with her. Ok everyone ready?"

I wave my hand and send them home. Hope it all works out for them. Is my last thought as I return home.

————————

Kyra

Boom! I land in my bed with a bang. Dizziness sweeps through me. My mind a whirl. I wait for it pass. I finally look around. I'm in bed. I'm home! I'm really home. My bed. My room. My house. I go to get off the bed and see the shattered lamp on the floor. I step over it. Looking around some pictures from the wall has fallen and they are scattered on the floor. But I'm really home.

I go to the living room and look around. It's dark so I go to turn the light on. It doesn't work. They turned the electric off. Shit! I go to grab a flashlight out of the drawer. I grab the broom and dustpan and a trash bag. I go to clean the house with a just a flashlight to light my way.

After all the cleaning is done. I go to take a shower. I grab my clothes and go to the bathroom. I turn the water on but all that comes out is cold water. Shit! So I hurry through a freezing shower and get dressed.

I notice my phone still on the charger. I check to see if there's any life on it. It's at fifty percent. Good. No messages. No calls. Nothing. There's nothing. As always. Nothing. I toss the phone on bed. I Look around. I grab my flashlight go back to the living room and stand in the center.

I hear cars outside and the echo of music from the bar at the back of my house. I see dust from the flashlight and sigh. I go to look for something to eat and all I find is a can of tuna and some crackers. I fix a glass of water and eat a tuna sandwich with a small bag of chips I left on the counter. I finish eating, clean up mess and stand to go back to bed.

I stand in my living room I look around again and cry. I cry. I break. I cry over the loss of them. I cry over the loss of what was my life. I just cry for what seems like hours.

I wipe my tears. I stand up from where I fell to the floor crying and look around again. I sigh, go back to my bedroom. I get under the covers. Turn off my now depleting flashlight and try to go to sleep. I'm home. I'm finally home and it's crushing me. I'm alone again. As always.

Welcome home.

———————————

Damon

Boom!

Im at the gas station. A bit dizzy. I take a look around. Fuck yeah! I'm back baby! I go in the station. "Can I use your phone?" I ask the clerk. A greasy looking guy with a ton of pimples. "Yea, sure" he hands me his cell. "Thanks" he just nods. I call Delaney. "Delaney man, I need you to pick me up at the Gas and Go." "Boss is that you? Where the hell you been man!" Delaney is my go to guy. Anything to do with my gang or my businesses he was there for me. Always has been. The only man I trust. Well; Was the only man I trust.

"I'll explain when you pick me up just get here." I hand greasy guy back his phone. "Thanks man" he just nods.

I run out to the lot to wait for Delaney. Ten minutes goes by and I see him pull into the lot. In my black suv. It's good to be home. I jump in and nod to Delaney. I then give him a hug. He looks shocked and eventually hugs me back. "You ok boss?" I laugh. I hard laugh. "I'm more than ok, let me tell ya what happened. Then we got some stuff do." I go to tell him everything. From where I've been. To our adventure and of course, Kyra!

We pull up to condo and get out. Everything looks the same. Delaney kept everything running like a fine oiled machine that he is. I sit on the sectional. Delaney follows suit.

"So what's the plan, boss?"

"Well first, I need to find a big house, at least six bedrooms, then my friend, I go get my lady." He laughs. I'm sure he's surprised at how much I've changed.

"Plus, I'm handing over the gang to you, Delaney. I'm done with it. I have my my clubs, the garages, and the hotels. The gang will be all yours." As I point to him. He's shocked. He's around my age. We've been doing this shit for years so I know he can handle it.

"Are you sure?" I nod my head "must be some woman?" He said then leans back.

"That she damn well is my friend." I laugh. Yes, I'm going to get my woman. Now, I just have to talk to the other guys and get this plan rolling.

I can't wait!

————————

Julian

Boom!

I land on my bed. Dizzy and shaken. Yes! Home sweet home! At last. I look around. The place is a mess. I jump out of bed. Turn on the light; then I clean. When I'm done I go to check my phone. I left it on the side table, charging. I look and I have 38 missed calls and 80 text.

The phone buzzes in my hand. Unknown number, I answer.

"Hello, Julian?" It's Jax. I remember I gave him number. "Baby boy is that you? We're home man, we're home. I can't believe it. Where are you?"

"I'm at the club, I'm on a pay phone. Can you come get me?" I hear music in the background. "Yea sure on my way!" I hang up the phone. Change my clothes and head out the door.

I'm so glad to be back. I can finally breath. I get in my truck and head to the club.

I love this town! I'm on a major high. It's good to be back. Now to get my job back and get in touch with Damon. We need to get our girl.

I can't wait!

——————————

Jax

Boom!

I land on a table in the club. Music is blaring and people around me are stunned. I guess I would be also if a guy plopped out of nowhere. I jump off the table a bit dizzy. I run to the bar.

"Gotta phone?" I ask the big barrel of a guy behind the bar. "There's a pay phone over there." He points to the far corner. "Thanks" I run to the phone.

Fuck! I have no change. I see a girl walking by. "Can I borrow some change? I need to make a call." I point to the pay phone. She smiles "sure thing stud" she winks and digs out some change from her purse. She tries to flirt, but I ignore her. Not my type. "Thanks" as she hands me the change and winks. Nope. Not interested. I turn to the phone. Dig out the paper with Julian's number. I dial.

"Hello, Julian? The music is loud. He answers I tell him I'm at the club and ask if he can come get me. I hang up the phone and head for the door.

I wait a few minutes and see a truck pull in. I run to it. I see Julian driving. Thank God. I couldn't wait to see him. I jump in as he stops and lean over to kiss him. He kisses me and we separated. We both have huge smiles.

"How bout we go get our girl?" He says. "I'm all in." I tell him and we head out. I can't wait to see Kyra. To make our family complete. "We should call Damon." I tell him. He nods. Damn I'm glad to be home. Now to get our babe and get our lives started.

I can't wait!

————————————Thank you pretties. Please vote and comment

TUCK

Two points of view. Enjoy!!

Boom!

I slam into my bathroom. I stumble, a bit dizzy. I look around. Yes! Home at last. I leave the bathroom and enter the bedroom and go straight for the living room. All the lights are on. It's a bit of mess but I don't care. As soon as I enter the room I see Chuck there on the couch. His hands are in his hair and his legs are bouncing. He turns to me when he hears me enter. He looks at me with eyes wide and he's stunned. I laugh and run to him. Engulf him into a huge hug. Patting him on his back. When we separated I see he has black circles under his eyes. There red and he's been crying.

"Where the hell have you been? I've been so worried. I've been staying here waiting for you. I found your phone so I know why you didn't call. I was all over Casandra wanting answers. I called the police. Even hired a private detective! Where have you been?" He starts crying. My brother is crying. I've never seen him cry. I hug him again.

"Sit down. We have a lot to talk about." He sits and i dive into my story. I tell him what Casandra did, about the realm, the guys, Tim, and her. I tell him about her. About what I put her through. About my ups and downs. About the sharing. I tell him how much I love her and how I was a damn fool. I spill my guts. I left nothing out. He listens when I tell him about how she sings. How she stole my heart. How she played my favorite song. I tell him about not using a condemn and how Julian and I got lost in the heat of it all. By the time I'm done it's almost early morning. We cried. We connected. We bonded.

"Ok so well what are you going to do now?" I don't know. I don't know how I'm going to win her back. How to show her how much I love her. I just don't know.

"I have no idea. Any suggestions?" He laughs. "Well first things first, you need to get ahold of these guys and talk it all out. Make amends, grovel if you have to. I'll help you. You will not have to do it alone." I don't believe it. All these years of competing, all those years lost. I look at him and it's like my life clicks into place.

"I can't wait for you to meet her."

"Oh brother I can't wait to meet her too. She must be some woman." Damn right she is.

"Well let's look the guys up. I'm too wired to sleep. Let's get this ball rolling." We jump up and go to my computer. I'm on the hunt. I'm home. I have my brother. I'll get a job. Get all the guys on board. Beg for forgiveness on my hands and knees if I have to and go get our woman.

I can't wait!

————————————

Two weeks later

"Ok so we all set?" Ask Julian we're in Damon's office, above one his clubs. My brother and I found all the guys and we've been having these meetings for a week now. Damon's been on the ball. The fucker bought a damn house. Seven bedroom house on the outskirts of town. He gave Julian his job back; but as head of all the male strippers. He gave me a job as head bouncer for all his clubs. The pay is phenomenal, I hesitated to take it but I couldn't turn down a dream job. He offered Jax a job but he declined; he is the prez of his MC and has plenty of money already.

My brother is here with us. He's been helping us through all of this. He basically hasn't left my side. I couldn't be more grateful for that.

He told me about the argument him and Casandra had at our olds man cabin. Kyra was spot on for every word of their fight. I should've believed her. I should've known how Casandra was. I didn't see it and I'm more the fool for it.

I did actually have to beg and plead for the guys to forgive me. It took awhile but with Chucks help; they eventually forgave me. Now to get Kyra to forgive me and agree to want we want. That's the tougher road. The guys have an easier path. Mine; not so much. I can only pray she will.

"How do you suggest we do this?" Ask Jax. We all look a bit rundown. Worried over what Kyra will say and all that we've had to do.

"I have no idea man." Damon says. He's behind his desk. He's been going nonstop; getting a house. Switching his gang roll over and getting us all situated. I don't think I cant thank him enough. He's done all this for us and her. He's a damn good man. Despite what he thinks.

"I may have an idea," said my brother. He's been my stone. My rock. We've grown closer and worked through our stuff. We've had a lot of late night talks lately.

"Ok tell us. Because I'm clueless." Laughs Julian he's the one that has organized most everything. Moving us all in into the house. Buying all the furniture and stocking Kyras room up to the hilt with clothes and what knots. He's like a machine when he gets going. He's been doing the decorating for the house. Just yesterday we finished it all. Just in time. I don't think we can wait any longer.

"Ok hear me out. I've never meet her but; from all the stories you've told me; I think I know how you can do this." He says with a huge smile on his face. The most friendliest guy you will ever meet. He fits right in to this crazy group of ours. I couldn't be more proud.

So he tells us his idea and we all agree it's the best of all our ideas. Now to get it all set up and get going. It may take a bit but it will be worth it in the end.

So we start planning. We want every thing perfect. We want our girl.

We can't wait!

————————

Kyra

So I sit here all alone. Waiting for the timer to go off. Praying it's a negative. I haven't heard from any of them. Not that I'm surprised. I finally got a job at the QuickMart. I registered again at my art school. I start classes next week. I got the utilities turned back on; after a week.

I've been working hard on all that. Till I'm behind the register yesterday and got really sick. I took off running to the bathroom and spewed everywhere. I was lucky I made it. My boss wasn't to happy;

but I couldn't help it. I bought a test on the way home. Now I'm waiting for the results.

I don't know what I'm going to do if it's positive. I wouldn't mind a baby. It would be a blessing. But I can barely afford to feed myself. I wouldn't be alone though. That's a plus. I'm always alone. It would be a good change. I tried finding their numbers. But without internet it's an impossible task. I know Damon owns clubs around town. But I don't want to show up begging for his care. It's just not me.

So I will go at it alone, as always.

The timer goes off. Here it's goes. I'm so nervous and really scared. I don't want to look. I'm terrified of the outcome either way. I stand up to go look then sit back down.

My mind is racing. I don't know of it could be Julian's or Tucks. I guess it doesn't matter. I'm the only parent the baby will have; if it's positive.

I can do this. I tell myself. I can take care of my baby and I will give the child a half way decent life. I will finish school and I will open my tattoo parlor. I will nurture my child and I will be a good mom. I stand up to go look and sit back down again.

Who am I kidding? No! No! I can do this.

I go to the bathroom and pick up the stick. Here it goes.

Positive!

Omg! I'm pregnant! What now? Now I have to make a doctors appointment. These test aren't always right. Right?

————————

One week later

"Well Miss Black, you are indeed pregnant." The doctor tells me and I cry. I just cry. The doctor gets all flustered and pats me on the back.

"I hope those are happy tears." He ask me. I look at him. He's an older gentleman. He's nice and understanding. How do I tell him what's going on? I straightened my back and wipe my cheeks. "Yes. It's happy tears." I tell him. He smiles and goes on about my prenatal vitamins and my ultrasounds. I zone him out. I nod my head all the while I'm freaking out on the inside.

He tells me goodbye and he will see me soon; I get dressed and head home.

I get home and throw my purse on the table and sit my couch. I'm not going to cry. I'm done with crying. I'm just going accept this and move on.

I go to fix me dinner. I'm tired; the traffic was awful and I'm so craving pizza. As soon as the pizza is done. There's knock on my door. That doesn't happen ever. I turn off the oven. I creep to the door and crack it open. There's a guy on my stoop with a chauffeurs hat and suit on.

"May I help you?" I ask. A little nervously.

"Are you Kyra Black?" He ask. I'm hesitant to answer. "Uhm yes." He smiles. He's older than me though not by much. He's cute. But I don't know him.

"Well Miss Black I'm here to escort you to Damon's residence. If you would just follow me please." He holds out the crook of his arm.

"Uhm, just a moment." I close the door. Damon? My Damon? It can't be. I look at what I'm wearing. I look awful. So I run to the bedroom and grab my white jumper and put it on. It fits me like glove. Showing off a bit of my curves. I go apply some make up and fix my hair. It's not perfect but it will do. I grab my phone and purse and open the door.

"I'm ready....Mr.?" He looks surprised.

"It's Delaney miss. Just Delaney." He said.

"Oh ok, just call me Kyra please." He smiles at me and I turn and see a limo. I'm shocked. I turn to Delaney and he laughs. He opens the door for me and I get in. He closes the door and goes to drive. Once he's in I ask "uhm Delaney...where is Damon's residence?" He turns to me "about 15 minutes from here. Just sit back and we will be there in no time. There's water or alcohol back there if you want something to drink. He turns and drives.

I look around and grab a water. I'm excited to see Damon. He reached out to me. He didn't forget about me. I'm so happy and overwhelmed. My day just got a bit better. I'm going to see Damon!

I can't wait!

————————

Thank you pretties. Please vote and comment Only a couple more chapters left. Who's your favorite character?Mines Tuck. Gotta love Tuck.

Jaxson

We're setting up the decorations around the house. Tuck is dropping the rose petals on the sidewalk. Damon is hanging the fairy lights. Julian is laying out the candles and I'm connecting the speakers.

"Do you know what song is going to be playing when she gets here?" Ask Julian as he places the candle. "Damon said Tuck picked it out." As I plug in the last speaker. We've worked on this for almost a week. Everything has to be perfect.

A car pulls into the driveway. Its Chuck. He's been helping out a lot. I like him. He's always smiling and friendly. He's a good guy. He's a firefighter. I don't know how he does that? He said you have to be crazy to do it. His motto is you have to be crazy to be a firefighter.

We're running to the fire, while others are running away. He's got a point there. Crazy fucker.

"I got the suits." He tells us. We go to him and grab our tuxes. This was Julian's idea. The tuxes. He really wants to make it grand. I can't blame the fucker. Anything for our girl.

"The lights are set"

"The petals are down."

"What about the song?" Ask Chuck.

"Got it ready. We got the song for the inside?" Ask Tuck

"All set, we just need to get dressed. They should be here soon." Damon says.

So we all go to get dressed. Even Chuck. I hate a damn suit. I can never get the tie right. Julian sees my dilemma and comes to help.

"You think this will work?" I ask him. I'm so worried she will turn and run away. We haven't contacted her yet we've been working hard on doing all this. We've had Delaney to keep an eye on her. We all want to surprise her. I'm a bit shaken up. Julian gets my tie all done and smiles at me. I kiss him. I have a surprise for him; but I'm nervous and have never done anything like this before.

"Uhm Julian, baby. I have something for you." He pauses putting his jacket on. I walk over to the drawer. I got it yesterday. I thought today would be the perfect day. I reach for the box and swallow hard. I turn with the box behind my back. I walk up to him. I get on one knee.

"Julian I love you. More than I could love any man. Any person; besides Kyra. I mean it's the same love but, I well...I can't picture a life without you in it." I bring the box around in front of him. I look up and he's smiling. Oh good. I'm a wreck. I swallow again. "Will you marry me, Julian? I promise to be a good husband; I will always be there for you. I will do anything to make you happy. So yea..,will you marry me?" I'm too afraid to look up. Too afraid he will say no. He grabs my chin and makes me look up. He smiles and says the two words that change my life.

"Yes! Yes!" I jump up put the ring on his finger and kiss him. I pour myself into the kiss. I give him all of me. I want to show this man how much I love him. How much I want to be with him. I feel something wet on my cheeks. I pull away and he's crying. He's crying! My beautiful and courageous man is crying.

"You ok?"

"Yea, I'm just so happy. I love you Jax. I will always love you." And we kiss again. We're almost complete now we just need our woman.

I can't wait!

———————————

Damon

I've worked my ass off for this moment. Blood, sweat, and tears. I'm not lying either. I had to kill to get out of the gang. It was well worth it. Delaney took over the reign. Our enemy is taken care of. We got the house. The crazy meetings. The days we heard Tuck apologize over and over again. The decorations. All of it and it will be so worth it.

I've had Delaney watch over Kyra for me. He said she's not doing so good. That she looks frail. She got her a job. But I'm going to the end that shit real fast. She doesn't need one; since she has us. She's back in school. Which is good. She needs that. I bought her a building so she can open her parlor. I have the equipment ready for her. She only has to sign the lease.

Damn! This fucking tie. I head over to see if Julian can help. I open the door and Jax and Julian are kissing. I wait. They don't notice me. They look good together. Their happy. Their just missing their piece of the puzzle to make them whole. We all are. I clear my throat and they break apart. Laughing.

Julian turns to me smiling. "Jax purposed!" He shows me the ring. Wow. Didn't think he had it in him. "Congratulations!" I tell them and I mean it. Their so good together.

"Now can you help me with this fucking tie!" He laughs and helps me. When he's done I look at them.

"I mean it guys, congratulations! I'm happy for you two." Jax says thanks. He's happy too. "Now we just have to get our woman." I so agree. I nod my head. "Y'all ready?" I want to get this show on the road. They nod and we go to find Tuck. I open the door and he's hugging his brother. Their both crying. It's an emotional day.

"Y'all ready?" They look at me and smile.

"Hell yea" Tuck says. We got to the parlor and grab the candles. Jax lights them up and Chuck turns off the lights.

"Turn the music on when she gets to the door." Tuck tells Chuck. He nods and heads off.

"You guys ready for this?" Ask Julian More than ready!

"Yes now be quiet, here she comes. We hear Delaney pull in.

We all get ready. Excitement running all through us. Then We hear the door open and the music begins to play. Here we go.

We can't wait!

——————————

Otter

I'm watching through the mirror. Keeping an eye on all of them. The councilmen are all around me. We're all excited and on the edge of our seats.

I've been watching them since they returned home. I had to explain why I did not erase their memories. So we watched them closely to make sure they keep their promise.

Drat! I was scared I was going to get sent to a prison realm. But I got lucky. Now we all watch it like it's a soap opera playing. We've watched the planning and struggles. Kyras misfortune and pregnancy realization.

We can't seem to get enough.

"Oh look she's walking to the door!" Councilman Treggan announces. He's a warlock. An old one. But he's so wise and happy all the time.

We all turn. Watching closely.

"I can't wait to see this." says councilman Darrius. He's always been a romantic. The vampire oozes charm.

"Pass me the chips." Says councilwoman Fiona. She's the head of the fey council. She's prickly but is in love with love.

"Otter where's my glasses I want to see properly." Says councilwoman Beatrix. Drat! There on her nose. For a werewolf she's completely blind.

"There on your nose you old bat!" Answers councilman Regar before I can. He's a dragon shifter and really grouchy. But I love working for all of them. They're a handful. But keep me on my toes.

Casandra it seems ended up being a real pain. Saying she did it all for love. Which piqued the councils interest. But as she got longer into her speech. The more the council despised her. She's banished for 100 years to the witch's realm. Serves her right. She's all alone. They won't allow her company for the way she isolated the others. Now she gets to feel the loneliness the others felt. They also stripped her of her magic. A fitting punishment indeed.

"Their walking in." I tell them.

"We know Otter!" They say in unison. Well drat! I was just telling them.

I lean closer to the mirror. I so want to see this outcome.

I can't wait!

TUCK

This damn tux! I hate a tux. I feel like a fucking penguin. Chucks laughing at me. He's use to wearing a tux, from the firemen formals. That's where he got the tuxes, from his buddies the Salvatore brothers. Their firefighters also.

"Need some help?" Chuck laughs. He's loving this too much. "Please" he comes to help me with the damn tie. The good man he is. He has helped plan all of this. He's just as excited and nervous as I am.

I need to find him someone who can make him happy; like I am. A woman who would be good enough for him. He deserves the best.

He finishes and ask "are you nervous bro?" Hell yes! I'm so nervous. She probably still hates me. I've done so much to her. Put her through so much. I don't deserve her. But I need her.

"Get out of your head. She will forgive you. How can she not?" He has faith in me. Faith I don't have in myself. If I only done things differently. I got to make it right.

We both agreed about Casandra. She deserves what she gets. She asked for it. He doesn't seem to upset by it. If I'd only talk to him sooner; none of this would of happened. But then I wouldn't have met the guys and Kyra. So I can't hate her too much.

"I'm sorry Chuck. For....everything." And I am. This all could of been avoided if I believed in him more. He never wanted Casandra. It was all in my head. The damn fool that I was.

"Stop! It's done. Let's move on. Don't rehash the past. You have the future to look forward too." He pats me on my back. Yes I do. But I want a happy one for him also.

"Why don't you come to the club. Let me find you a girl. You deserve the best Chuck." He laughs. Always the happiest in the room.

"Nah, I'm good. Thanks though. I have a certain taste in women. Besides this night is about you. Not me. Let's concentrate on that...for now. " he smiles. That I will. He's been so good to me.

"Chuck...thank you for...all of this. You're the best brother a man can ask for. You mean the world to me. I want you to be as happy as I am. As we all are. You deserve to be happy." He starts crying.

"Bro, I love you, come here man." He hugs me. Tight. Now we're both crying. We hear the door open. We turn. The guys are standing there in their tux. They look good.

"You ready?" More than ready.

"Hell yeah!" And we head out to get ready.

We can't wait!

————————

Kyra

The limo stops. Delaney gets out and opens the door. He peeks his head in "you ready, princess?" I nod my head and exit the limo and stop in my tracks.

There's fairy lights in the trees in front yard. In front of a massive two story house. There's rose petals all on the sidewalk and little lanterns lighting the way. There's a song playing through the speaker. Open Arms. I pause. It can't be? Tucks here? Julian?

"Go ahead." Delaney urges me on.

I slowly walk to the door. I open the door. It's completely dark. I close the door. There's a song playing in here drowning the other song out. It's Eternal Flame, oh no, I start crying. I promised myself I wouldn't cry again.

There's no one around.

"Hello"

There's a flickering light coming from the arch way. Jax walks out holding a lit candle. He's dressed in a black tux. Handsome as ever. He looks at me and smiles. He goes to the end of the room; in front me.

Next is Julian. He holds a lit candle in a blue tux. Sexy and smiling. He goes and stands beside Jax, smiling. I start to say something. Then.

Enters Damon holding a candle in a black leather tux. Stunning. He's smiling. He goes to stand on the opposite side of me. Right in front. I go to speak again but then

Tuck enters holding a candle in a grey tux. He's smiling but he's nervous. A beautiful beast still. He goes to stand beside Damon. They group together in a line in front of me. They all start singing. Their singing for me Eternal Flame. Im crying. This is all for me.

They pick up a rose each. In different colors. Damon hands me a red one. Julian hands me a yellow one. Jax hands me a multicolored one and then Tuck hands me a white one. They go back in line and they finish the song. I'm melting.

Jax speaks first.

"Kyra, I love you. With everything in me, I love you. You are my sun and Julian is my moon. You are my light. You make my heart flutter. I am nothing without you. You are my temptress.

Then Julian

"Kyra, my cookie. I love you, you are my sweet on a lonely day. You are my world. You fill me up and make me beyond happy. I can't breath when I'm not with you. You are my reason for air. You are my heartbeat.

Then Damon

"Kyra my spitfire, you are my legacy. I love you with all my heart and soul. You're my present, my future, and my ending. You are what makes me. You are a diamond amongst the rocks. You are the fire that burns in me.

And last Tuck

"Kyra sugar, I'm so in love with you. I'm so sorry for all that I have done. I will make it up to you; even if it takes me a lifetime of apologies and showing you everyday how sorry I am. You are my queen. The love of my life. There is no other but you and there never will be. You are my dream come true.

All together they ask

Will you marry us?

Tuck has a box in his hand. He opens it. It's a gold ring with four bands. There's a heart shaped diamond in the center. I look up to the men of my life. I go to stand in front of Jax.

"Yes" he jumps up and kisses me.

Julian"Yes" he does the same.

Damon"Yes" he kisses me also.

And finally TuckI look him in the eye. He stands up. Worry all over his face.

"Yes" he kisses me. Screams "hell yeah!" And puts the ring on my finger.

I can't believe it. They love me. They want to marry me. I will never be alone alone again!

"Uhm guys there's just one thing." I stare at them. They stop and look. All of them show concern and worry. I'm scared to tell them. What if I lose them? What if they don't want to be dads?

"I'm pregnant"

"What? Yes we're gonna be dads?" Julian screams and laughs and hugs me.

"Yes" screams Jax and hugs me and kisses me.

"Damn. Bout time." Said Damon. He kisses me and hugs me.

"Hell yeah!" Screams Tuck. He lifts me off the ground and twirls me. Then kisses me.

Their all laughing; the questions come all at once.

"How far along?"

"When's the ultrasound?"

"Are you ok?"

"Do you need to sit down?"

I just laugh. I'm so happy.

They keep talking over each other.

"We have to fix up a room for a nursery."

"Is it a boy or girl?"

"We need to go shopping."

"Are you craving anything?"

"We need a crib!"

"Can I pick out the name?"

Awe my guys. I couldn't ask for anything more. They are my world.

Then someone clears their throat. I look around Tuck and see another Tuck! He's smiling. He has longer hair but they look so much alike.

"This is my brother Chuck, Chuck this is Kyra." Said Tuck. Chuck walks up to me and shakes my hand. I look him in the eyes and smile.

"Hello, I've heard a lot about you, dimples." He said and smiles. He has a dimple too. I laugh.

He's charming and not like Tuck at all. Though I love Tuck. Have to love the grumpy too.

"I've heard a lot about you too." He leans down and kisses me! He kisses me! Oh boy, am I in trouble. He grabs me by my hips and brings me in closer. I feel his hardness against me. He breaks away from me and smiles again. I'm a goner. I smile back. The guys laugh. I have my family. I have my loves. I have my heart. My loves.

I have all four. But....

There's always room for one more. I turn and look at Chuck.

————————

CHUCK

Ten years ago if you would of told me that I would be married, I would of slapped you! Yet here I am. Married to Kyra. So is my brother and three more.

We're the happiest people in the world.

When I saw her I was blown away. Her beauty. Her smile. Her dimples. I heard so much about her from Tuck that I just fell in love. Fast and hard. We added another gold band to the ring. We also had an unofficial wedding ceremony in the backyard. She was dressed in white. Her gown showed her delectable figure; with only a slight pudge in her stomach. Her hair has was flowing freely. She held a multicolored bouquet and she looked amazing. She's legally married to Damon though. We thought it was the best option.

Tomorrow is our anniversary. We have a sitter for the kids. We're going to take her the beach and renew our vows. She has no idea.

We have four kids. Two boys: twins. Bobby and Robert. Their ten and a handful. Just like me and my bro. We have two girls. Kayla is seven, she looks just like Julian. He spoils her rotten.

Our other girl is Kelli she's five. She looks like Damon. She is a spitfire.

We're expecting another one. She's eight months. This one is Jax there's no doubt in that. The guy refuses to use a condemn. It's a boy. He wants to name him snake but Kyra won't let him. I think they decided on Charles. That makes me happy. She wants to have mine next. I'm not going to argue. I would love to have a child of my own. If it's a boy I would name him Presley and a girl would be Cristy. At least that's what we agreed on.

"Baby you ready?" Kyra ask. More than ready.

"Yes, dimples. Almost, is Tuck home yet?" She wobbles over to me. She's stunning pregnant. She has a glow and it's mesmerizing. We're waiting on Tuck to get home for dinner.

Tuck walks through the the door as I ask. He swoops Kyra in a hug and kisses her. "Hello sugar, how's the baby?" He rubs her belly. He's a changed man. He's rarely angry anymore. He works hard and very affectionate. I'm proud of him.

Jax and Julian are staying out tonight to celebrate their anniversary. They officially married a day before we married Kyra.

"Man, I'm starving, how are you spitfire?" He kisses Krya and rubs her belly also. He's a very happy man. He guards her and hardly lets her out of site. She finished art school and opened her tattoo parlor that he bought her. She oversees it now. She occasionally does a tat or two. But the kids keep her busy.

She comes over to me and kisses me. I can't get enough of this woman. She's my everything. After I kissed her that night. We went out on a date. The others didn't mind. She ask me to marry her too on that very date. I was shocked. But there was no way I was going to say no. The love bug hit me hard. I never thought I'd share a woman either. But here I am. Sharing a woman with my brother and three others. It's amazing. I wouldn't change a thing.

"You ok?" She ask me while she rubs my face. I smile. I couldn't be more ok.

"I love you so much dimples." I kiss her again.

"I love you too." She hugs me. Her belly rubs against me. I feel a kick. She looks back with wide eyes and we laugh. Jax would be so happy. He hasn't felt him kick yet. It pisses him off that he never catches it.

I look at Kyra and grab her hand. We sit down to eat.

My world is almost complete. She's having my child next and I'm beyond happy.

I can't wait!